Courting Calla

Dixon Brothers Series Book 1

by

HALLEE BRIDGEMAN

Published by
Olivia Kimbrell Press™

Olivia Kimbrell Press™

COPYRIGHT NOTICE

PUBLISHED BY: Olivia Kimbrell Press™*, P.O. Box 470, Fort Knox, KY 40121-0470. The Olivia Kimbrell Press™ colophon and open book logo are trademarks of Olivia Kimbrell Press™.

Olivia Kimbrell Press™ is a publisher offering true to life, meaningful fiction from a Christian worldview intended to uplift the heart and engage the mind.

Some scripture quotations courtesy of the King James Version of the Holy Bible. Some scripture quotations courtesy of the New King James Version of the Holy Bible, Copyright © 1979, 1980, 1982 by Thomas-Nelson, Inc. Used by permission. All rights reserved.

Original Cover Art by Amanda Gail Smith (amandagailstudio.com).

Library Cataloging Data

Bridgeman, Hallee (Hallee A. Bridgeman) 1972-
  Courting Calla / Hallee Bridgeman

  186 p. 5 in. × 8 in. (12.70 cm × 20.32 cm)

Description: Olivia Kimbrell Press™ digital eBook edition | Olivia Kimbrell Press™ Trade paperback edition | Kentucky: Olivia Kimbrell Press™, 2017.

Summary: Can Ian and Calla find love together, or will the secret she is keeping rip them apart?

Identifiers: ISBN-13: 978-1-68190-111-4 (ebk.) | 978-1-68190-112-1 (POD) | 978-1-68190-113-8 (trade) | ePCN: 2017959951

1. clean romance love story 2. women's inspirational 3. man woman relationships 4. Christian living 5. identity theft debt 6. forgiveness redemption 7. secrets and lies

Courting Calla

Dixon Brothers Series Book 1

by

HALLEE BRIDGEMAN

This book is dedicated to my husband Gregg's grandmother, Calla. Thank you for stepping in and being a loving maternal figure in the wake of his mama's death. I know how much he loved you and how much he still misses you.

This book is also dedicated to the missionaries from Vision International who work at the real orphanage in Ti Palmiste upon which I modeled my fictional orphanage. Thank you for your love and dedication to Christ's Great Commission that pours out onto the orphans in your village, and for the example of love and servitude that you give to us all.

May God bless your service.

Hallee Bridgeman

TABLE OF Contents

CHAPTER 1

alla Vaughn felt the telltale shudder of the car through her seat just as she started to pull through the gate. "No, no, no," she said out loud, as if the machine might actually hear and decide not to die in the middle of the post-lunch rush to the parking deck. Despite the feeble attempt to stop it, with a lurch and a cough and a cloud of black exhaust, her car sputtered to a stop.

Resigned, Calla slipped her glasses off and lay her forehead on the steering wheel, closing her eyes, the smell of burning oil stinging her nose. If this week would just end, if she could just get through this afternoon, then tomorrow, and make it to the weekend, everything would turn out fine. It had to. Surely, the domino effect of her life would still and cease if she could just shut the door to her little apartment and hide from the rest of the world until Monday.

The tapping on her window startled her, and she hastily sat up, slipping her black-framed glasses back on. She knew with her black hair and dark brown eyes the thick black frames made her face stand out. She'd resisted buying them, but Sami, her best friend and confidante, had insisted, claiming they gave her a striking appearance. She said the glasses made her look like she just needed a nearby phone booth to transform into a courageous and strong heroine in primary colors. Calla knew nothing could help her not ugly but certainly not beautiful features, but she kind of wanted to see if the new frames would change her life in any way. They hadn't, of course. They were just glasses. So much for wanting to look like a superhero in disguise.

As she rolled down her window, her face flooded with uncomfortable heat. Of course, the car behind her would belong to Ian Jones, one of the mechanical engineers in the Dixon Contracting firm where she worked as a file clerk. She saw his signature a dozen times a day in her job but hadn't ever spoken to him beyond an uncomfortable hello whenever they passed in the halls. He had bushy brown hair, light hazel eyes that shifted from gold to brown to green, and a face better suited to some rakish Duke in one of her favorite Regency romance novels. She'd carried a crush for him since her second day on the job three years ago, though he barely glanced at her whenever their paths happened to cross.

Trying to keep from actually crying out of embarrassment, something that would make this whole horrible moment a thousand times worse, she simply drawled out, "Hi there."

His right eyebrow rose and his lips twitched up into a half grin. He had a dimple. "Need some help?"

If he only knew. The fish and chips lunch she had just wolfed down started to feel like bad sushi. She smiled weakly and asked, "Do you have a tow truck handy?"

He looked at her little Geo Storm that had rolled off the assembly line the year she was born and tapped the sun faded yellow roof. "Put her in neutral. We'll just move it out of the way of the gate." He gestured with his head, and she looked in the rearview mirror to see the growing line of cars behind them. She watched him wave an arm, and another man got out of a car three cars back.

With a sinking, burning feeling in her chest, she recognized him as one of the Dixon sons. She suddenly started wishing she believed in portals that would open up and suck someone into another dimension. Mr. Dixon, owner of the massive Dixon Contracting construction and architectural firm, had three identical sons. Triplets. No one could really tell them apart, so they were all simply "Mr. Dixon." She guessed this was Jon from his pickup truck but honestly had no idea whether maybe one of his brothers, Brad or Ken, had borrowed Jon's truck this morning.

The little Storm shifted when Calla felt Mr. Dixon's hands grip the sooty back bumper. Following Ian's directions from the driver's window, she put her car in neutral and glanced out the window in time to see Ian's biceps bulge and bunch beneath his shirt as he maneuvered the car while Mr. Dixon pushed. "Let's get it to that spot there," he said, and she turned the steering wheel as they propelled her into the senior Mr. Dixon's space.

As soon as she set the parking brake, she hopped out of the car. "I can't park here. Mr. Dixon—"

"Is nowhere near Atlanta today. He's inspecting the New Orleans job for at least another three days. You're fine. Don't worry about a thing," the young Dixon said. He smiled, clearly trying to put her at ease. Turning to the man next to him, he said, "Hey, Ian? You're next, bro."

As the two of them rushed back to their cars that still sat blocking the entrance through the gate, she lifted a hand at their retreating backs. "Thanks." It sounded weak even to her own ears.

Sighing, cheeks burning with embarrassed heat, she pulled her phone out of her purse intending to call a garage. Her hands shook slightly from chagrin and, as the phone cleared the purse, it slipped from her fingers and crashed to the concrete parking deck floor. A flood of tears blurred her vision, making the cracks that appeared on the screen all blur together.

"Calla!" She looked up with tear-stained cheeks as Sami's zippy little convertible pulled up next to her and her best friend put her head out of her open window. Sami's eyes went from Calla's face to the ground next to her feet, then she put her car in park, and hopped out. "Oh, Calla, honey, let me help." She bent and picked up the broken phone, slipping it into her own pocket. She had on a brightly flowered shirt, mustard yellow leggings, and red boots. Somehow, with her blue fedora sitting on top of perfectly curled black hair, it worked. "I'll call my uncle. He has a garage in Decatur."

"Don't bother. I couldn't pay to fix it, anyway. I'll just get it towed to a junk-yard. It's where it belongs."

Sami raised an eyebrow. "And then what?"

Realizing she had started to grit her teeth, she intentionally relaxed as she closed her eyes and took a deep breath and held it. In with the good, out with the bad. Letting out a long, slow sigh, she said, "Then I ride the Metro until I can get out of the hole my stepmother has so graciously dug for me." She reached into the pocket of Sami's shirt and snatched her phone. "I'll be fine."

"You'll get out of that hole faster once you press charges," Sami said. When Calla opened her mouth to protest, Sami held up her hand. "I know. I won't say it again. That's between you and God and the local police." She looked at her watch. "Get back to work. No reason to add trouble at work to your load. I'll take care of this.

I have personal time saved, and you don't."

Calla hugged her, tightly, knowing God had blessed her with a true friend. She retrieved her bag from the back seat, made sure she didn't have anything in the glove box she didn't need, and rushed to the elevator just as Ian Jones reached it. Feeling the clumsy awkwardness that he always invoked overtake her, she smiled an uncomfortable smile and pressed the button for the second floor. "Thank you. Sorry to block your way."

He turned to look directly at her. "Glad you had a small enough car that it was easy to move. What brings you to Dixon this morning Ms…?"

She stammered a reply, "Vaughn. Calla. Calla Vaughn." Realizing Ian didn't even know her name made it even worse. Did he think she was married? "It's, uh, Miss. Not Mrs." Had she really just said that? "Not Miss, either. Don't call me Miss Vaughn. It's just that I hate that Ms. nonsense and I'm not married. So I'm not Mrs. Vaughn. But don't call me Miss Vaughn. I mean…" She closed her eyes one heartbeat after she shut her mouth. She took a breath, exhaled through her nose, raised her head, smiled, and said, "Call me Calla. And I, uh, file."

The dimple had reappeared. Throughout her entire babbling introduction, he hadn't so much as moved. He cleared his throat and nodded. "You file?"

"Here. I file here. At Dixon. I, uh, work in the file room."

"Ah." He nodded as the elevator stopped on her floor. When she just stood there, he held the elevator door open with his left hand and gestured with his right hand. "I believe the files are that-a-way."

She glanced through the open doors and saw the oversized glass doorway that provided access to the rows and rows of filing cabinets surrounding the cluster of cubicles. "Right," she said, stepping off the elevator. "Thanks. Uh, thanks for everything."

He extended his right hand toward her and said, "My name is…" but when she placed her fingers lightly into his right palm he stopped speaking.

"I know who you are, sir," Calla whispered, trying not to think about how nice his fingers felt beneath hers, though staring at his dimple didn't distract her from that thought very much. She jerked her hand back and stepped further out of the way of the elevator doors. "I see your name all the time."

"Right." He acknowledged. "Well, you're welcome. No problem at all." He gave her a single wave goodbye just as the doors slid shut.

After the doors slid closed, Calla took a final deep breath. In with the good and out with the bad. After she slowly released it, she reluctantly headed to her little cubicle and put her purse in the bottom drawer of her desk. Next to her desk, a large cart from the architectural division sat, piled with papers, plans, and files. Knowing that would take up the rest of the afternoon, she slipped earbuds into her ears, maneuvered through the broken screen on her phone to access her favorite radio station's app, and started sorting files.

Samuel Ian Jones thought about Miss Calla Vaughn and her big brown eyes the entire trip from where she left him on the second floor all the way up to the seventh floor. As he walked off the elevator, he tried to rid his mind of the worry and stress he saw in her eyes and focus instead on the amount of work he had to do in the next three hours before his four o'clock meeting. He crossed through the empty conference room that took up the center of the floor then maneuvered through the cubicles used by the interns and assistants. He went straight to his office on the far side from the elevators. He left the door open, knowing his assistant Penny would arrive bare seconds behind him.

Pulling his phone out of his pocket, Ian set it on the wireless charger, then used the remote control sitting next to the charger to turn on his favorite classical radio station. Only then did he allow himself to go to his coffee maker, choosing an English tea over a coffee pod. After confirming that he had no messages waiting in either office voice mail form or email form, he grabbed his fresh brewed tea and sat on the stool at his drafting table. Before he even picked up his pencil, Penny slipped inside and shut the door behind her.

"Your four o'clock canceled. The incoming storm has them closing down the site early."

"Do I need to go now?" he asked, thinking of the twenty-story building in the heart of downtown. The weekly job site meeting was a vital part of the construction process at this point in the schedule.

"No. They want to try to arrange a phone meeting

with you and the architect first thing tomorrow morning. The full job meeting stays at the regular time next week."

"So just fast-tracking this week? Good." He felt an immediate release of stress over what he needed to accomplish since he'd just added two extra hours of useful work time to his schedule.

She gestured at him. "You have something black on your shirt."

He looked down at the white golf shirt he'd worn to work and saw the streak of oily black dirt. "Hmph. Must have been the Storm."

Puzzled, Penny asked, "I beg your pardon? The storm's miles away. Where did you eat lunch, exactly?"

"No, not that storm." Unbidden, his thoughts once again returned to Calla Vaughn. She'd come across as utterly hopeless, which was silly considering they got the car moved within seconds of it breaking down. Maybe she just didn't know what to do next. The Mister-Fix-It inside of him thought about looking her up in the company directory and calling her, making sure she could handle the arrangements. Maybe he could give her a ride home. Maybe they could stop for a bite on the way. He quickly talked himself out of it. That would ruin his self-imposed moratorium on helping any people under the age of sixty. Well, unless said people happened to have a broken-down car blocking the path to his parking spot. "Never mind. Anything else?"

"Yes. You received a phone call from someone who claimed it was important but addressed you as Sam. Since only your grandmother ever calls you anything but

Ian, I figured it was a vendor. I took the number, anyway." She held out a slip of paper.

As he took the note from her, he chuckled. One nice thing about going by his middle name, he always knew when someone actually knew him or when they looked at his name in some directory and tried to pretend. "Thanks, Penny."

"Sure. Let me know if you need anything. I'm leaving at two, today, don't forget. And I'll be out all day tomorrow."

"Right. Long weekend at the beach with the potential husband. I remember." His own moral compass never entered his relationship with Penny, who happened to be a fantastic secretary despite her personal lack of faith and resoundingly secular worldview.

As Penny shut the door behind her, he looked down at the dark streak on his shirt one more time then shook his head, reminding...no, telling... telling himself to stay out of it. Instead, he unrolled a set of plans onto his drafting table and focused on the mechanical engineering for the shopping mall Dixon Brothers had contracted to convert into a megachurch.

By the time three o'clock arrived, the sky outside Calla's cubicle window had darkened, and it looked more like nighttime than afternoon. She could see the branches of the trees across the street bending and bowing in the wind. Her phone had alerted her twice about thunderstorm warnings, and she thought about the wet walk from the metro station to her apartment she faced this evening. Resigned, she punched holes in the papers in her hand and fastened them to the prongs of the file folder in front of her. Inevitably, she would get soaking wet tonight. She tried to remember if she had an umbrella somewhere in her apartment; not that it would do her any good tonight. Still, since she had to ride the train for a while, she should probably have one on hand.

Even through the love song playing in her ears, she could hear the rain pelting against the windows. She began praying that the storm would move quickly through the area and completely dissipate before she had to go home. Maybe she could put in some overtime work. She certainly had enough work to do, and she really could use the extra hours.

Before she could go to her supervisor Francine and ask, her desk phone chirped. She slipped the earbud out of her ear as she answered the phone. "File room, Calla Vaughn," she said by way of greeting.

"Hey, girl," Sami said. "I'm driving you home tonight, but first we're going to get loaded on nachos and *pollo* enchiladas," she announced, accentuating the word *pollo*. "My treat. No arguing. See you at five."

Before Calla could reply, Sami hung up. Relief at not having to walk in the weather warred with the desire not to take Sami up on what was clearly a charity offering.

Wait, silly, she thought to herself. This is Sami. It's

not charity. It's a friend acting like a friend. You'd do the same thing.

Just as those thoughts left her, the DJ on the radio announced, "Next week is Thanksgiving. Crossroads Florists has teamed up with us here at Q103 to let you send someone special in your life a beautiful fall bouquet. Caller number ten will be our winner this hour. Four-oh-four, five-five-five, Q-one-oh-three. Caller ten."

Phone still in hand, she dialed the number. Her heart leaped when she heard it ring. "Q103, you're caller four. Good luck next time!"

They hung up without another word. Calla hit redial. To her surprise, she could hear the phone ring again. "Q103. You're caller ten! Congratulations! Who do we have on the line?"

Mouth dry, heart pounding in excitement, she said, "Calla."

"Well, Calla, you've won a bouquet of fall flowers from Crossroads florists. Who do you think you'll send them to?"

Calla smiled. "Actually, I know exactly who deserves a bouquet."

I an listened to his desk phone ring but ignored it while he typed details about the limitations of the customer requested heating system into the project's specifications. He had a two o'clock meeting about this project and didn't have time to do Penny's job. As he had pulled in this morning, he felt somehow unexplainably disappointed that Mr. Dixon's parking space sat empty. He had sort of hoped to catch a glimpse of a faded yellow Geo Storm parked there, which made no sense and had him wondering exactly where that thought even came from.

He had made it all the way up to the seventh floor today before remembering that Penny had the day off. The morning hours jumped from one crisis to another. For some reason, everything always erupted on Friday morning, as if everyone had sudden onset panic attacks over the prospect of no one working for the next two days. With Penny out, it made everything outside his office door feel like chaos.

As he finished typing, he didn't even look up at the sound of a tap on his door. "Come," he called, sending the print order for the specifications he'd just written to the print department before closing the lid of his laptop. He expected an intern or even his friend Al. When a large bouquet of flowers in the colors of fall came through his door, he raised an eyebrow, confident the person belonging to the legs he could see under the arrangement had come to the wrong office.

"May I help you?"

"Delivery for Sam Jones," a squeaky teenage boy's voice said.

Curious, he got up from his desk and removed the mammoth bouquet from the boy's arms. "Okay. Well, thank you," he said absently.

"Happy Thanksgiving," the young man said as he ducked out of the office.

Who would send him flowers? More importantly, who would send flowers for him addressed to Sam? His grandmother? Definitely not her style, but maybe her assistant did it without guidance? She usually wouldn't send such an elaborate bouquet full of sunflowers, mums, chrysanthemums, roses, dahlias, and gerbera daisies. He dug through the stems until he found the envelope that contained the card clutched in the prongs of a transparent plastic fork. The scent of the roses filled his senses as he opened the envelope and read the typed note.

CAN'T THANK YOU ENOUGH FOR YESTERDAY. YOU WERE A LIFESAVER. DINNER AT MY PLACE. SIX TOMORROW NIGHT. WON'T TAKE NO FOR AN ANSWER. WANT TO THANK YOU PROPERLY. CALLA

Ian cleared his throat, a little embarrassed and uncomfortable at what he had just read. The last time a girl had so boldly asked him out was for high school homecoming dance senior year. How did he even respond? Should he respond? Should he just not show up?

Then again, maybe he should show up. Admittedly, he had thought of her more than once since their encounter and elevator ride yesterday afternoon. He had fleetingly entertained the notion of asking to give Calla a ride home and maybe treating her to dinner last night. Still, this seemed very forward on her part, much more forward than he would have expected based on their brief conversation. Highly unexpected, surprising, and a little bit unsettling.

What did one do with something like this?

Should he just ignore it all together? That felt rude.

Should he return the flowers? Even more rude. She didn't deserve rude. Maybe just shoot her a short email, or give her a quick call down in filing. Just let her know that he had appreciated the offer, but that the flowers and the gratitude they expressed were thanks enough. No. She had sent him flowers. His response had to be equal to that gesture and an email or even a phone call would seem too impersonal, really.

Besides, did he really want to decline? He found Calla very attractive. Also, and of equal importance in his mind, he assessed her as a genuinely nice person. What would be the harm in accepting her invitation? Even if things didn't work out, it might get Al off his back for a while. That would be nice. Of course, she worked for the same employer as he did, and that could spell trouble in the future. Interoffice romances always came with extra challenges. He really didn't have the time to deal with interoffice drama, much less any inclination.

Deciding he would have to speak to her in person, he glanced at his watch. He had a few minutes before his meeting began. He would stop by the file room on his way to the print department and politely respond to her invitation.

Even as he walked out of his office, though, he had no idea what he would actually say to Miss Calla Vaughn. As the elevator arrived on his floor, he decided that unless he saw some very compelling reason to join her for dinner, he would smile and politely let her down. Hopefully, she would take it well.

Calla strode, skipped, and hopped to the beat of the song playing in her ears, holding a file folder in each hand as she hummed, spun, and swayed to the tempo. Her eyes closed as she performed a stage-worthy pirouette then popped open a file drawer with a hum and a low whistle. She expertly inserted a red file folder into the drawer then rhythmically bumped the drawer closed with her hip and a Rockette flourish before dancing further down the aisle.

Halfway through a turn, she faltered, and stopped moving entirely when she identified Ian Jones standing at the end of the row of filing cabinets. She must have looked even more odd standing there in a frozen vignette pose with just her eyes widening and no other discernable movement, like a New Orleans street mime, maybe. How long had he stood there, watching her? Feeling her face flush with heat, she straightened, yanked the earbuds out of her ears, and cleared her throat. "Uh, sorry. Just, you know, keeping it fun."

His right eyebrow sat higher on his forehead than his left, but the left side of his mouth curled into a dimpled half-grin. "Fun, huh?"

Her voice sounded weak to her own ears. "It's, uh, kind of quiet and a little cave-like in here. Music makes the day go a little faster." She shoved the earbuds into the shirt pocket that contained her phone and adjusted her glasses on her face. He just stared at her with that half a smile on his face.

"I see."

She set the file folders on top of the closest cabinet and walked toward him. Thankfully, he hadn't come three hours ago when papers, hole punchers, and files had covered the floor. "Oh! Can I do something for you? Penny usually comes for files, but I just remembered she's out today."

His eyes widened slightly. "You know Penny?"

She shrugged. "Well, I know all the assistants. They come here to get files and, you know, there's just the four of us down here." She kept a thin pad of paper in her skirt pocket and pulled it out with a pencil. "What can I pull for you?"

As she reached him, nervousness came over her that made her hand tremble a little around the pencil. Why, oh why, did she become such a bumbling, stuttering, fumbling idiot around this man? Why couldn't she act poised and calm? Why couldn't she look three inches taller and twenty pounds thinner? And maybe more classically beautiful. Without the glasses.

Ugh.

He just stared at her, with his head slightly tilted. She began to wonder if she had something on her face. Finally, she said, "Mr. Jones?"

He cleared his throat. "Ian. Please, just Ian. So, about dinner."

She tilted her head slightly toward him, unconsciously mirroring the angle of his gaze, and raised her eyebrows as if trying to hear what he said better. Was he? No. She must not be understanding him. "Dinner?"

"Yeah, dinner. Tomorrow. Your place. Remember? Flowers? Invite? Won't take no for an answer dinner?"

Flowers? Invite? Dinner? "Uh…" Suddenly, she realized.

Samuel Ian Jones. Sami Jones.

Oh no! Remembering what she'd put on that card, her whole face flashed with molten heat and she carefully set the pencil down on the counter before she dropped it. Oh no! "I, uh…"

"I just need your address. Not sure I can make six, but I can do my best to make six-thirty or so if you're on this side of town."

He was accepting an invitation to dinner from her? Not that she had actually invited him to dinner. Well, he thought she had invited him. Still. Why in the world?

Deciding not to sound like more of an idiot than she already had every time they'd spoken, she mumbled her address and confirmed that six-thirty would be great. He had the grace not to cringe about her wrong side of the tracks address. Out of habit she asked, "Is there anything you won't eat?"

Ian's face lit up in a smile. It made Calla's heart thump against her chest so hard she thought he might hear it. "That's really nice of you to ask. How about this? I promise I'll eat whatever you put on the table. I'm not what you would call a picky eater. But I've never really been a huge fan of shellfish."

Calla nodded and said, "Okay, so omakase is for sure off the menu."

"Oma-what?"

"Omakase." Calla said, carefully pronouncing the Japanese and bowing slightly. "It's, like, the most expensive shellfish dish on earth. You can only get it in this one place in Tokyo… you know what? Chef joke. Never mind. No shellfish. Got it."

She hadn't thought his smile could get bigger, but somehow it did. He had very straight, very white teeth. He glanced at his watch and took a step back. "Can't stay and chat. Gotta run by the print department and pick up some plans for a meeting I'm nearly late for. I'll see you tomorrow, though. We can talk more then?"

"Sure," she said weakly, "tomorrow. Dinner. My place. Looking forward to it."

As soon as she was sure he wasn't going to return, she rushed out of the row and told her supervisor she was taking a late lunch. Forget that hour of overtime she'd planned on, she needed to talk to someone!

In no time, she found herself on the eighth floor ensconced in Sami's little office outside Brad Dixon's office door. The big boss was with his dad in New Orleans, so she felt safe sitting down across from her desk. "You'll never believe what just happened."

Sami rolled her chair closer to the edge of her desk and leaned forward. Her bright green eyes shone out from under a metallic green gypsy scarf that she'd tied around her head. "Spill."

"So, yesterday I called in and won flowers from Q103."

Sami's eyes widened. "Seriously? Cool! I won a gift card, once."

"Yeah? Anyway, perfect timing because you'd just called me, offered to buy me dinner, and arranged for my car to be towed to the junkyard. You totally saved my life last night. Really. And I knew you would. So, I preemptively sent you a thank you bouquet."

"Me?" Sami grinned. "Wow! Thanks! I hope I get them today!"

"That's the thing. They were already delivered." Nervous and edgy again, she said in a voice barely above a whisper, "To Sam Jones."

A frown appeared between Sami's eyes. "Sam Jones? Sam?"

"Yeah. Sam. Samuel Ian Jones."

With wide eyes, Sami said, "Ian? The hot guy on seventh you've had a slightly obvious crush on since you started working here three years ago?"

Mouth dry, she cleared her throat. "Yeah. That Ian."

Sami threw her head back and laughed. "So, he got your flowers. What happened next?"

"You mean after he read the card thanking 'him' for his help yesterday and demanding that 'he' come to dinner at my place tomorrow so I could thank him properly?" Calla used air quotes for the him and he. "Why, he came down to my little forest of metal filing cabinets to ask me for my address so he could come have dinner and get properly thanked."

Sami's mouth opened and closed twice before she said, "Seriously? Calla!" she said her name on a gasp. "Isn't God good? That is amazing!"

"What am I going to do?"

"What do you mean, what are you going to do? You're going to do what you do in the kitchen and make something amazing. I have no doubt."

"Yeah. Sure. In my dinky one-bedroom apartment that doesn't even have a table! I was planning on making you spaghetti and garlic bread. Cheap. Easy. Filled with love and gratitude that you would have understood. Him? He wears a watch that cost more than my car is worth! How am I supposed to cook for him?"

Sami started to answer, but her phone rang. She held up a finger and answered the call. She scribbled a few notes and said, "Yes, Mr. Dixon," she paused, "right. Give me five minutes."

She hung up the phone and turned to her computer, bringing it out of hibernation. "I can't think right now, Calla, but I have a table you can borrow. We'll cover it with a beautiful cloth, and you'll do something amazing. I'll be over at ten in the morning."

"Sami!" Calla pleaded.

Sami shook her head. "Honey, this is a good thing. A very good thing. Stop worrying. It'll be fine. Now shoo. Let me work."

Calla stood as Sami began maneuvering through the

files on her computer. She lifted a hand to wave goodbye as she left the office.

Ian shifted under the weight of his end of the dresser and waited for Al to guide the way. His feet remained steady on the gold-colored shag carpet as they maneuvered the massive chest through the little World War II era cottage.

"Step at the door," Al announced, and Ian started expecting the feel of the metal threshold that would clue him to take a step down. As soon as they cleared the doorway, they turned sideways and moved with more precision and speed, soon setting the dresser into the moving van.

Al, a well-muscled six-five electrical engineer who dedicated four mornings a week to the gym, looked like he'd barely broken a sweat. Four inches shorter and a good thirty pounds lighter, Ian felt the strain in his arms as he rolled his head on his shoulders.

"Bedroom's done," he said to Daniel, the leader of his church's men's ministry. "Are the guys ready to start loading the kitchen boxes?"

"Pretty sure," Daniel said, using a handkerchief to wipe the sweat at his white hairline. "Let me go check with Marlene and I'll let you know. Why don't you two get some water and take five?"

Ian wouldn't admit to how relieved he felt at the suggestion. He followed Al over to Daniel's truck and grabbed a bottle of water out of the cooler in the back. As he twisted the cap open, he sat on the open tailgate. He looked up through the branches of the live oak tree and saw the vivid blue of the Atlanta sky. The dry seventy-degree temperature made it a really lovely November day.

"Want to grab a pizza after?" Al asked. "Georgia's playing at seven, and that place in Decatur's going to show it on every screen."

Fast friends since the first day of engineering school at Georgia Tech, Ian and Al spent most weekends doing something together, either sharing a meal or two, catching a movie or a football game, or something casual and relaxing of the sort. However, right now Miss Calla Vaughn dancing to the tune in her ears floated across his mind. "Actually, I have a date."

"A date?" Al's teeth looked bright white against his chocolate colored skin as he grinned at his friend. "Well, well, well. About time. With whom, may I ask?"

"Calla Vaughn. From work."

Al frowned and muttered, "Calla Vaughn? Is she in the architectural division?"

"No. She's one of the file clerks down on the second floor." He took a long pull of water. "I helped Jon push her dead car out of the way of the gate reader Thursday afternoon. She's cooking me dinner to thank me all proper like."

Al threw his head back and laughed. "Your grandma would love that one."

Ian pressed his lips together as his rather blue blood heated. His grandmother, old member of Atlanta high society, would certainly not find amusement at Ian's dating anyone other than a crowned princess, perhaps. Or maybe a president's daughter. Depending, of course, on whether said president drank red or blue Kool-Aid.

"It's not that bad," he lied.

"Oh, please," Al said, "she's the reason you don't ever date."

Ian raised an eyebrow. He couldn't deny it. It was just easier not to date than to try to find someone who would pass inspection and gain the reluctant approval of the family matriarch. "Yeah? What's your excuse, then?"

Al's face sobered, and he cleared his throat. "Like you don't know."

Feeling like a cad, especially as the brother of the woman who so thoroughly broke his best friend's heart two years ago, he immediately apologized. "Dude, sorry."

"No sweat." Al looked up when the door to the house opened, and a very small, frail woman carefully maneuvered her doorway with her walker. "Need help Mrs. Manchester?" The church men's group had volunteered to help move Mrs. Manchester's belongings into storage while her son got her settled into his spare bedroom.

"You boys get on in here and get yourselves a

sandwich," she ordered. "I made egg salad. Even managed to toast the bread before the toaster got packed."

"Yes, ma'am," Ian replied, standing.

"Did you make some of your sweet tea?" Al asked, a hopeful sound in his voice.

"You better believe it." She turned and carefully lifted her walker back into the house. "Ain't nothing like egg salad and sweet tea."

"No, ma'am," Al agreed. Ian laughed while he followed them slowly into the house.

CHAPTER 3

"**B**eautiful," Sami assured, surveying the rust-colored tablecloth covering the little square table, the short round vase filled with bright sunflowers, and the white plates perched atop gold chargers. She arranged one of the rust-colored napkins more carefully in the sunflower napkin ring and stepped back, putting her hand on the back of the folding chair. "Thank goodness for the dollar store. Who knew, huh?"

"You did," Calla smiled, looking at her living room transformed into a very welcoming dining room. "You do so well with this kind of thing."

"It's not hard. You just find a theme or a color scheme and go with it." She turned and looked around the room, nodding at the throw pillows she'd tossed onto the worn brown couch. Their colors perfectly matched the tablecloth and napkins. "I'll pick the card table and pillows up tomorrow after church," she said, "where I intend to get the full scoop about every word that gets spoken tonight."

Calla's stomach dropped in a nervous flutter that had grown in intensity since waking up this morning. "Maybe he won't show," her voice sounded weak. "He's a gentleman, after all. So polite all the time. Maybe he'll spare me the humiliation of acting like a total idiot tonight."

"Nonsense," Sami replied. She followed Calla into the kitchen. As Calla pulled an onion out of the grocery bag on the counter, Sami rummaged in the refrigerator then shut the door and looked at her. "Okay, bread is rising, I see chicken and spinach in the fridge. What else is on the menu?"

Calla looked at her watch and calculated the time she had left in the day. "Chicken Florentine served on a bed of wild rice and some fresh green beans." She lifted the towel covering the loaf of bread and pressed into it lightly with a knuckle of her little finger, deciding to preheat the oven. As she turned the dial to the right temperature, she added, "I'm just doing some fresh berries and whipped cream for dessert."

"That sounds lovely." Sami picked up her purse and pulled her car key out of the side pocket. "I can't wait to consume leftovers after church tomorrow."

Calla walked over to her and hugged her. "Thank you for your help. You have calmed me considerably."

"I loved the project. I especially loved the project on such a budget. It was a challenge and kind of exciting."

After she left, Calla went back into the kitchen and pulled a skillet out of her cabinet. She ran her finger over the ceramic coating on the inside of it and felt a small smile. Her couch might have seen better days ten years ago, and her car might have died completely, but no one looking at her kitchen accouterments would ever think that she bought anything but the very best for herself. She thought about the three semesters of culinary school she'd attended, where she had never felt so alive and free in her life. One day she would go back. As soon as she got everything in order in her life, she'd have the freedom to walk back into the school and don her apron.

She heated some olive oil in the skillet while she quickly sliced an onion and some garlic. When she heard the oven signal that it had reached the desired temperature, she slid the bread inside and set the timer. As she did, she marked the time and knew everything was right on schedule.

Ian approached the apartment, looking around as he walked along the concrete breezeway. From the second floor, he could glance down over the metal railing and see the dirty swimming pool with a few faded plastic chairs scattered around it. He passed apartment 2C taking in the broken blinds hanging crooked in the window. He reached 2D, Calla's apartment according to the address she gave him. Light cotton curtains adorned her windows.

The area in front of her door looked swept clean, and a mat bid a "Welcome Friends" greeting. On either side of the door, pots filled with fresh herbs covered tiered plant stands. Some he recognized, like the massive bush of rosemary. He smelled mint and parsley among other scents he could only guess at. Oregano, maybe. All of the scents mingled and filled his senses with such a pleasant aroma that he wanted to just stand there and breathe it in deeply. He held his finger over the doorbell and hesitated only slightly before pressing it. Within seconds, Calla opened the door, and the first impression he had was the tantalizing smells coming from the apartment that even overpowered the scent of the herbs.

Then he took in the sight of her. Calla wore an oversized rust-colored shirt that buttoned with brass buttons all the way down to her thighs, dark leggings in a geometric design with rust, mustard yellow, and forest green colors, and knee-high brown leather boots. Yesterday, she'd worn her sleek black hair down, swinging to her shoulders. Today, she had it pulled back in a ponytail, which made those rich brown eyes behind those large black framed lenses stand out even more.

"Hi," she said, smiling, "welcome. You're exactly on time."

She opened the door wider, and he stepped in, quickly surveying the room. Bright pillows on the couch and the small table covered with an autumn flare gave the room a happy, homey feel. He spotted a little desk in the corner with a laptop, lid closed, sitting on top. With the flustered way she'd acted when her car broke down and the way she floundered and fumbled when he went to see her in her department yesterday, he halfway expected a little bit of chaos in her environment. Not so. Even the desk looked neat and ordered.

"Part of me wondered if you would even come." She shut the door behind him, and he noticed that she almost absently locked the deadbolt.

"I thought about it. It's not every day I'm invited in such a fashion." He slipped his hands into his pockets. "The table's beautiful."

"Thank you." She touched the back of a chair. "My friend Sami came over and helped. She has an eye I don't have. I'm better in the kitchen than in the drawing room, I'm afraid."

His stomach gave a slight rumble of hunger and his mouth watered at the thought of the heavenly smells. "I can't wait to compare."

She walked into the kitchen, but it didn't place her out of his sight or hearing. He moved to the small bar that separated the two rooms and watched her use a kitchen towel to pull a pan out of the oven. He saw roasted chicken breasts bulging with a spinach stuffing.

"That looks amazing," he said.

"I hope you like spinach. I probably should have checked." She took two plates out of her cupboard and set them side-by-side on the counter. After lifting the lid of a pot on the stove, he watched as she scooped wild rice onto each plate, then placed one of the chicken breasts on top of the rice. Using tongs, she artfully arranged green beans alongside the chicken. He couldn't help but notice the confidence and smoothness with which she moved while she handled the food. She picked up each plate and walked back into the room, setting them on the little table. "I hope water's okay. It's really all I drink after six," she said, picking up a clear pitcher of ice water off of the bar. "I can make coffee or tea? I have decaf."

He shook his head. "Ice water's perfect."

Where did these nerves come from? He was twenty-eight years old. It's not like he'd never had dinner with a beautiful woman before. But suddenly, he found himself anxious, worried he'd say the wrong thing, move the wrong way. He suddenly longed for that moment when the initial awkwardness passed, and he'd relax around her.

She gestured toward the chair nearest him, and he waited for her to settle into her chair before taking his. Following her lead, he pulled the napkin out of the flowered napkin ring and laid the cotton cloth across his lap, setting the ring to the side of his silverware. She started to pick up her fork then set it back down. "I'm sorry. I feel wrong eating without praying. Do you mind if we pray first?"

He smiled in reaction to the question, a smile that revealed his straight white teeth. "I'm actually relieved to hear you say that." Automatically, he held out his hand to her, palm up. She didn't so much as hesitate as she lay her hand in his and bowed her head. His fingers enveloped her slim hand gently, and she gave his hand a little prompting squeeze. Waiting for half a second to make sure she didn't intend to lead the blessing, he spoke, listening to his voice fill the otherwise silent room. "Father, we thank You for this food. We ask that You bless it, bless the hands that made it, and let our fellowship be pleasing to You. Amen."

As soon as they lifted their heads, he felt himself relax, somewhat surprised that his initial attraction to this woman just increased with her desire to pray before the meal. "This looks really good," he said, slicing into the bird with his knife. The aroma and the juicy tenderness of the perfectly prepared and well-portioned entree compared to the finest meals he had ever enjoyed. "I could smell it as soon as you opened the door."

She smiled, conspicuously pleased with the compliment. "I'm glad. This is a favorite dish of mine." Her eyes widened, and she tossed her napkin atop the table and quickly stood. "Bread!"

She rushed into the kitchen and returned with a basket that she set on the table in front of him. When he opened the napkin on top, he revealed a pile of steaming hot sliced homemade bread. He selected a piece and smiled. "Bread is a good thing."

"It felt good to knead it this morning. It's one of the ways I like to relax. Is it good?"

Amazed that she'd made her own bread, he took a bite and almost closed his eyes in wonder. As he savored the light yet hearty perfection of the bread, he shook his head slowly from side to side. Finally, he swallowed and answered, "No." Calla looked slightly panicked until he said, "No, I would describe it as excellent. Not just good."

Relief washed over her expression, and her shoulders relaxed as she reached for a slice of bread for herself. "This is a really good whole grain flour. It's better with fresh ground flour, but I don't have my own grain mill yet. Saving up for it, though. There's a wonderful place to get grain over on the west side of town."

"Fresh ground or not, it's delicious. Anytime you feel stressed and need to work it out by kneading some bread dough, please know that I'll happily take any extra loaves off your hands."

Her laugh rang around the room. "Deal."

He took a few bites of the amazing chicken dish before he spoke again. "How's your car doing?"

The frown that crossed her face made him wish he hadn't asked the question. "Totally dead. I'm car-less for a while. Thankfully, there's a MARTA station on this block and one near the office, so I'll be okay."

"I think it would be hard to function in Atlanta without a car."

"Unless there's a wreck on the 300. Then it's hard to

function in Atlanta with a car." She grinned.

He chuckled, thinking of the main road dead stop traffic of every weekday rush hour in and around Atlanta. The bigger Atlanta grew in any direction, the more improved the infrastructure, the worse it seemed to get.

She shrugged. "Not much I can do about it anyway." She poured herself more water. He noticed she didn't eat with the same enthusiasm he felt for the meal. "Sami will give me a ride wherever I need to go, if there's somewhere I can't get to by train or bus. I'm totally fine with it. Besides, it'll save me the insurance payment every month, so there's that."

He considered her words, wondering if he could help her in any way. Then he had to remind himself that he'd officially given up on helping people not formally classified as an elderly person in his church. Not even a sabbatical anymore. More like a life choice. Officially. Period. End of story.

Still…

Calla sat against the opposite arm of the couch with her legs pulled up under her, her body turned toward Ian, cradling her coffee cup in her hand. He sat on the other end. When he'd arrived hours before, she thought she'd come out of her skin with nerves. She'd opened the door, and there he stood, like something she'd dreamed about since the first time she saw him walking the halls at Dixon Contracting. His hair had shown damp traces of a recent shower, and she could smell his aftershave when he'd walked into the apartment. Tonight, the dark-green button-down shirt made his hazel eyes shine a bright green.

Despite her initial nerves, they enjoyed such a relaxed and enjoyable meal. She felt relief she never gave in to her weak impulse to cancel the dinner and just admit to Ian wires had crossed and she never intended to invite him in the first place. After finishing the chicken, she served them fresh berries with a basil infused whipped cream. She probably should have toned down the cheffy foodie-ness of the meal, but the look on his face when he took the first bite made her glad that she'd stepped outside of what most would consider a normal boundary.

They enjoyed their dessert on the couch—much more comfortable seating than the metal chairs at the card table.

"My best friend, Al, and I are the young, single, and in shape men in our church. So, we call it volen-told. We get volen-told a lot. We get *told* that we *volunteered* for most tasks that involve heavy lifting. I think I've had a free Saturday morning twice in the last four months."

"What was this morning?"

"Helping an elderly widow move into her son's place. We packed her house up into a storage container. So, we had one truck going to the son's, and another to the storage facility." He set his coffee cup down on the table next to them, and she noticed he hadn't had more than a sip or two. "She's a sweet woman. Her son is quite old himself, and they have no other local family, so the church stepped up to help her."

"What would you do on a normal Saturday if you didn't have to help an elderly widow move? Rescue cats from trees? Feed orphans?"

He grinned and shrugged. "In the spring, I'm on a baseball team. We always play on Saturdays. Al's talked about wanting to find a basketball team for the winter months. But, I'd rather just stick with baseball. I tend to hole up in the winter. It's about the only time I allow myself to indulge in long stretches of reading for pleasure and not for work or education. I have a hoop at my house, and Al and I play one-on-one every so often, but I'm not really into being on a team."

Thinking of the bulging bookshelf in her bedroom, she perked up. "I love to read! I wish I had more time to do it. What do you like to read?"

"Fiction? I like thrillers. Medical mysteries." He smiled. "Sometimes Biblical fiction, if I like the author."

"I like cozy mysteries. You know, the kind where the sweet old woman who owns the little tea parlor somehow stumbles upon a murder and works out the killer by having one-sided conversations with her cat?"

He stared at her blankly for a moment then threw his head back and laughed. "I can honestly say that I have never read anything like that."

"They're brilliant. I cut my teeth on Agatha Christie

novels, and the insight and intelligence of Miss Marple always stuck with me. Whenever I come across a good character like that in a series, I'll read every book the author has written in just a few days. It's crazy." She gestured toward the desk. "I work a lot. Evenings and weekends, I caption movies and television shows, so when I intentionally take off to read, it's about all I do."

She watched him look at her desk and back at her. "Caption movies?"

"Yeah, you know. Like the closed captioning."

"Huh. How'd you get into that?"

Remembering the process, she decided not to bore him with the details. "I wanted something I could do early mornings or late nights to earn a little extra money. A friend told me about this website, so I applied. I type really fast, so that helps."

"That's actually kind of fascinating." He looked at his watch and shifted forward. "It's later than I want it to be. Better call it a night. Thank you for an amazing meal, Calla."

She set her coffee cup down and stood as he stood, then gestured toward the door in a nervous movement—as if he may have forgotten how to find the front door. He unlocked the deadbolt and turned to face her. "I really enjoyed talking with you. I'd love to take you to lunch tomorrow. Maybe you could go to church with me, and we could have lunch afterward? I'm happy to give you a ride."

Her heart beat a little bit faster. He wanted to spend

more time with her? "I ah, have a church. I teach the preschool Sunday School, so I can't come to church with you. But lunch would be very nice."

They discussed where and when to meet, and then he opened the door. Did she see hesitation in his eyes? A reluctance in his movements? For just a fraction of a second, it looked as if he might reach for her, but the moment passed. She put her hand on the doorknob and smiled. "I really enjoyed cooking for you, Ian. Good night."

C alla sat in the back row of her church and felt her cheeks burn with shame. She hated the sermons about offerings, tithing, and giving. No matter what she knew in her heart or her internal desire to tithe, she struggled to the point of drowning in debt so she couldn't possibly do it. How could she give ten percent of what she had when what she had was negative forty-six thousand, seven hundred according to last week's calculations? She looked around feeling like everyone knew this about her, even though no one possibly could.

If only she could fix it. She thought about her situation and felt anger brimming on the edge of rage burn in her heart, the kind of anger she hadn't felt in a long time. Maybe it burned because she had such a good night last night, perhaps because she knew that, eventually, Ian would find out. He'd find out and then what? What would he think? He certainly wouldn't want to have anything to do with her afterward.

Trying to push back the anger, grief pushed through, and sad tears pricked her eyes. She pulled off her glasses and pressed her fingers against her eyes. Her father's death had come as a surprise. Her stepmother's betrayal came as more of a shock in the wake of his death.

Three years had passed. One might think she would have recovered from the shock and accepted the reality of the situation by now. However, sitting here in the back of the church with all of these thoughts running through her head, her heart suddenly overwhelmed, she found herself on her knees in front of her pew sobbing. She felt hands on her shoulders and heard whispered prayers, but she didn't look up to see who ministered to her. She just started praying from deep inside her soul asking for God's help and release from this pain. Petitioning to Him as Jehovah Jireh, God her Provider, for provision to fix it and make it go away, begging Him for wisdom to know how to help herself through this trying time.

When the storm of emotions passed, she felt empty. Not exactly empty, more like hollowed out. Her stomach felt cold, swirling with a winter wind, and a cold sweat covered her skin. Her hair clung to the back of her neck, and she reached back and lifted it off, feeling the cool air conditioning. She stood and hugged the woman who had prayed with her, knowing she knew her name but unable to retrieve it from the chaotic thoughts swirling in her mind. She thanked the woman for her prayers then snatched up her Bible and purse and slipped out the door.

Calla had planned to meet Ian for lunch, but she wanted to cool off first. She didn't want him to see the evidence of her crying jag. She walked down the street to the restaurant a full thirty minutes before they arranged to meet and slipped into the bathroom. She saw her reflection in the mirror and realized she looked as bad as she thought she would with her bright red nose, puffy lips, and swollen and red eyes. A little trickle of a tear slipped out of the corner of her right eye and slid down her cheek. She frowned with impatience at the fact that she still had more tears inside. Thankful for the little makeup kit she carried in her purse, she turned the cold water on in the sink and let it wash over her wrists, cooling her down.

Her text tone sounded as she finished drying her face. She slipped her glasses back on and glanced at the sender. Sami. She would have seen her escape from the church from her position in the choir loft. The message read:

FIGURED THAT SERMON WOULD GET YOU. CALL WHEN YOU CAN. ENJOY YOUR LUNCH.

Calla typed out a quick reply thanking Sami and glanced at her face in the mirror again. She had cooled off a little. The cold water helped. The ugly cry face had started to fade away. After reapplying her makeup, she brushed her hair then pulled the sides of her hair back from her face and clipped them with barrettes. Her bright red dress and polka dot red and white scarf had made her feel happy this morning. Thinking of her lunch date with Ian, she chose bright colors over more muted fall tones. She smoothed her hands down the side of her dress and checked her reflection in the mirror, turning this and that way, then grabbed her purse and Bible and walked out of the ladies room.

She entered the lobby area of the restaurant just as she saw Ian come to the door. Since she'd just seen him last night, the joy at seeing him walk through the door surprised her. She'd walked him to the door of her apartment about twelve hours ago, but for some reason, it felt like a lifetime had passed. He wore khaki pants, a blue dress shirt, and a dark blue blazer. The blue turned his eyes a brown-gray. He'd unbuttoned his top button, and she could see the end of his tie hanging out of his jacket pocket.

Maybe God had done something in reply to her desperate plea earlier. Maybe something inside of her head changed. Whatever the case, she felt a big grin appear on her face the moment she saw him. When he saw her, his eyes lit up with a smile, and she easily went into his arms for a hug.

"For some reason, I feel like it's been a lifetime since I saw you last," he said.

Her eyes widened as she grinned and said, "I was just thinking that exact same thing. I had a very ugly crying deep prayer at church and wondered if it was just something that happened to me there, or something else."

She waited while he spoke to the hostess then stepped forward as he gestured toward her. He put a light hand on the small of her back as they followed the hostess to the little table next to the window. She felt acutely aware of the feel of his fingers through the fabric of her dress. As he pulled out her chair, she glanced out the window to see a family walking down the street pushing a baby carriage. Despite the late November day, the mid-sixties temperature outside made a Sunday stroll in the downtown area a pleasant time.

Ian studied her for a few moments before he remarked, "Ugly cry at church, huh?"

She felt a tiny bit of emotion creeping back into her throat, so she took a sip of her water to get herself back in control. She gave a small shrug of her shoulders. "Sometimes sermons get the best of me. It's hard to know the right thing to do is if you don't happen to be doing the right thing at this exact moment."

He raised a questioning eyebrow. "Like what?"

"Like anything." She paused then paraphrased the book of Romans. "There's not one righteous. No, not one."

Just in time, the waitress approached. She was blonde and young and very bubbly with a sparkling green bow in her hair and bright pink lipstick. "What can I get y'all?"

She hadn't even glanced at the menu. Ian never even opened his. He said, "I'm ready. Do you need a few minutes?"

"No." Looking at the waitress, she said, "I'll take a turkey sandwich and a side salad with the house dressing on the side."

Ian scooped up her menu and handed them both to the waitress as he said, "Burger, medium well, extra mayo. Fresh veggies on the side. No fries."

The waitress nodded, wrote down the orders, and asked, "Anything more than water to drink?"

Calla shook her head. "I'm good if you can bring me some lemon."

Ian smiled. "I would love some of that good iced tea." As the perky blonde walked away, he looked at Calla again. "What is your testimony?"

She could have thought of a dozen questions beyond that one. It stumped her. "I beg your pardon?"

He sat back in his chair. "Your testimony. What has God brought you from? Where is He taking you?"

A server brought a small dish of lemons, and she took the opportunity to contemplate her answer as she added two slices to her water. "I went to a youth group with a friend when I was fifteen. I knew when I left there that night that I'd changed. My home life was hard. My mom died when I was three, and my dad remarried when I was fourteen. His new wife was one of his college students. She acted like a bratty stepsister instead of a stepmother. So, I went to this youth group party, and my friend introduced me to Jesus. Home life changed overnight."

Ian smiled. "I like that."

She waited, but he didn't say anything else, so she finally asked him. "What about you? What's your testimony?"

"Orphaned as a teen. Fourteen. My paternal grandmother finished raising me. She's old money, so, like my father before me, I grew up in a staffed household and attended private boarding schools. But, she is also a devoted follower of Christ and serves Him like no one I've ever seen. All of my uncles work with her, and their various businesses help support her in whatever she needs for her ministries. Our family Christmas vacations are spent in Haiti at an orphanage, and Easter is down in Ecuador. We don't do a lot of traditional American holiday things save Thanksgiving and Fourth of July.

"As I entered adulthood and realized the true uniqueness of my upbringing, I found myself in awe of my family's faithfulness and often pray I can live up to it." He sat forward and folded his arms on the table in front of him. "I love Dixon Brothers Contracting because they're as mission-minded as my grandmother. But, I also like going to my own church, away from my family, and creating my own legacy instead of living in the shadow of hers."

She let what he said sink in, then slowly nodded. "I can see that, even if I have no actual experience with it." The tension from leaving the church service dissipated as she leaned forward with her elbows propped on the table and put her chin in her hands. "I wish my dad had come to know God before he died. But, he never did. Not that I know of, anyway. And, I assume if he did, I'd have known."

Ian's eyes sobered. "That would be hard. I'm sorry."

"It made everything about his death harder." She smiled warmly. "Two orphans. Too bad it's not raining out there. I'd make some poetic reference about finding each other in a storm."

He reached forward and put a hand on top of her arm, giving her a gentle squeeze. "There are all different kinds of storms. I'd say that would be accurate despite how warm and bright it is outside. After all, it was a Storm that brought us together."

Knowing he referred to her car, she smiled warmly. A server approached with their meal, and they both sat back to give room for their plates. As soon as she refilled waters and walked away, Calla put both of her hands in his. He asked, "Would you like to bless the food?"

Clearing her throat, she bowed her head and felt heat flood her cheeks as she softly thanked God for providing safe harbors in the storms of life, and for their food. When she said, "Amen," he gave her hands a warm squeeze before releasing her fingers.

Cold wind and rain drove Calla into the building. As the glass doors shut behind her with a whooshing sound, she shook her umbrella over the rubber mat and pulled the damp collar of her coat closer to her. She couldn't feel the heat in the building until she walked further away from the doors and into the lobby. She couldn't believe how fast the weather had changed from yesterday to this morning. Thankfully, she'd found an umbrella in the back of her closet and hadn't had to walk from the train station without one. As she approached the elevator, she felt a hand on her elbow and looked to see Ian standing right next to her. Immediately, a bright smile covered her face as the joy in seeing him lit her up from the inside. Her reaction surprised her, considering she'd seen him just yesterday at lunch.

He wore a cream dress shirt with black and yellow grid lines and a tie covered in the Georgia Tech yellow jacket mascots. Somehow, he made that look classy and stylish. Even in the crowded lobby, the scent of his aftershave tingled her nose.

"I was hoping I'd catch you early," he said with a warm smile.

"Good morning," she greeted. She pulled her glasses off to wipe the rain from the lenses.

"I know your shift starts at eight, which means you still have about twenty minutes. Would you like a cup of coffee?"

He'd sought her out—waited for her in the busy lobby on a Monday morning. She knew he typically began work at six-thirty, so his presence in the lobby could only be intentional. A warm rush of emotion moved from her chest through her whole body, making her face flush.

"Coffee would be heaven right now," she agreed, wondering if she might have said it a little too enthusiastically. They got into the elevator, and he pushed the button for his floor. As they moved up, stopping at floor after floor, the crowd gradually thinned until just a few people shared the car with them. When they stepped off the elevator on his floor, he put a light hand on the small of her back to guide her. They strolled through the empty conference room in the middle of the floor to the sea of cubicles and desks, then on to the other side, where he unlocked an office door and she stepped into his realm.

Motion sensors caused the fluorescent lights to flicker on. On the far wall, bookshelves on either side of a credenza held thick tomes of books on engineering and architecture. His desk sat in front of it, empty except for a phone and a black leather desk pad. Next to the window, she saw a small counter that contained a single cup coffee maker and a water filtering pitcher. Across from the window on the other wall, she saw his drafting table with a closed set of plans sitting on top of it. A rack of plans sat on one side of the table, and a low shelf full of bound specifications sat on the other side. A whiteboard with various columns and notes written in different colors hung above the table on the wall. She recognized job numbers, dates, and some codes.

He moved directly to the coffee pot on a counter and put a ceramic mug under the spout. With efficient movements, he placed a coffee pod into the machine and, within seconds, the smell of brewing coffee filled the small room and made her mouth water. She already felt warmer.

"How was your Sunday evening?" she asked as she slipped off her damp coat. Underneath, she wore camel colored wool pants and a brown sweater. She wiggled her toes in her boots, thankful that her feet hadn't gotten too wet.

"It was quiet," Ian said. "I watched highlights of the ball game and readied myself for the week. Yours?"

"The exciting life of laundry." She grinned. "I don't know why I always put it off until Sunday night. I captioned a thirty-minute television show in between loads."

She noticed the massive arrangement of flowers sitting on the credenza behind his desk. Immediately, she felt a little guilt and walked over to it, running a finger over the petal of a mum the color of the richest wine. "Ian, I have a little confession to make," she said quickly before she could talk herself out of it.

He brought her the steaming mug of coffee, and then went back to the coffee maker to wait for his cup to brew. "A confession? That sounds interesting."

She cleared her throat and took a sip of the coffee, hoping the hot drink might give her a little bit of courage. "Yeah, a confession. I hope you're not, ah, angry."

"Impossible to tell with this much information. I'm going to have to digest it." His teasing tone helped boost her fortitude. His coffee finished brewing and he pulled the cup out from under the spout and took a careful sip.

She took a deep breath deciding that the longer she kept from telling him, the worse it would be. "These flowers," she said, then she stopped, cleared her throat, and continued, "the flowers were meant for my friend Sami." With his blank stare, she elaborated. "Sami Jones. Brad Dixon's secretary. I don't know how the delivery company got them to you, except it may be because your first name is Samuel. Anyway, I'm sorry I didn't tell you when you came to my office Friday, but I was kind of in shock and really, really wanted to have dinner with you."

He stared at her for several seconds, not moving, and she couldn't read his thoughts behind his stoic expression. Finally, he sent his coffee cut down and walked toward her. "I think," he began his voice low and deep, "that if you had said this to me on Friday afternoon, I would have been annoyed and embarrassed. But because I have spent so much time with you this weekend, all that I can say is I'm thankful to God for that mistake and believe very sincerely that this must be something He orchestrated."

With everything he could have said, she did not expect *that*. He reached down and took her hand and didn't say anything. He stood close enough that she could feel the heat from his body, and just looked up at him, staring into his hazel eyes. He reached up and slipped the glasses off her face.

A tap-tap on his door made her step quickly away. She clasped her hands behind her back and watched annoyance creep into his eyes at the interruption.

"Hey, Ian? Just got word that the 9:00 got moved to

8:30," Ian's secretary Penny announced as she came through the door. She stopped short when she saw Calla standing next to Ian behind his desk. He very casually handed her glasses back to her. She fumbled and almost dropped them, but finally got them back on her face.

Comically, Penny didn't speak until Calla had her glasses back in place as if she didn't recognize her without them. "Oh, hi, Calla."

Heat flooded Calla's face, and she stepped even further away from Ian. "Hi, Penny. Good morning."

She wanted to escape, but she still had almost ten minutes left and didn't want to miss the time with him. Instead, she scooped up her coffee cup and clasped both hands around it.

"Thanks, Penny," Ian said. He paused. Penny paused, looking back and forth between him and Calla. Finally, he asked, "Anything else?"

Penny smiled and stepped back out the doorway. "Nothing that can't wait," she said through her grin.

Ian turned and looked at Calla as the door shut. "Sounds like the day has to begin," he said.

"Pity that." At his grin, she burst out laughing. "I hope there comes a time when I'm not so nervous around you."

"Well, I'm terrifying. I don't blame you for feeling nervous." The dimple appeared.

"Not terrified. But I am nervous. I admit it."

"You'll get used to me. We just have to spend more

time together." The cell phone on his desk began vibrating at the same time his desk phone started chirping. "Lunch?"

"I brought mine, but I'm happy to share." He had a hand on each phone, so she set her cup on the credenza next to the flowers and waved at him. "Get to work. Come get me when you're free." As she slipped out the door, she found Penny hovering, obviously waiting for her.

"Do tell," Penny said, grinning. "I'm dying to know."

"Penny," Calla whispered, looking around, "Shh." She knew all of the secretaries well because they all constantly communicated with her about files. She and Penny had hit it off as friends almost immediately. "I can't. Really. Too new." But she stopped and leaned her back against the door and put a hand over her heart. "But, I have to say, I feel like I'm walking on air."

Penny waved her forward and grabbed her hand, pulling her into an empty conference room.

"I interrupted something, didn't I?"

"Maybe." She thought about what might have happened after he took her glasses off. "Fine. Yes. But, really, it's so early. Please..."

"Girlfriend, I love Ian second only to my boyfriend. And, well, maybe my brothers and dad. But he's up there. I wouldn't hurt him or gossip about him to save my life." She laughed and brought her clasped hands up to her chest. "But I feel so happy right now! It's like perfection to me."

Calla looked at her watch. "I have to get downstairs. Catch up with you later. You still need to tell me about your weekend getaway."

Penny grinned like someone clutching a secret. "Oh, I do. I can't wait."

Calla laughed and rushed to the elevator, making her way down to her floor. As she walked to her desk and slipped her purse into her drawer, she watched the digital clock on her radio switch to 8:00 exactly.

"Good morning," Francine, her boss, greeted, coming up behind her with a stack of requests. "How was your weekend?"

"Wonderful," Calla sincerely replied. "Best one I've had in a long time."

"That's fantastic." Francine held out the papers. "Best get to it. The short Thanksgiving week has everyone trying to cram the world into three days, and Meredith and Becky are both out this week."

Calla took the papers and walked over to the empty counter that spanned the length of the room. She started sorting requests. With dozens of rows of filing cabinets, documents cabinets, and plans racks, she needed to sort by department—legal, accounting, residential, commercial—and by location inside the filing system. Once she had everything in order, she pulled the plans, blueprints, and specifications first, and loaded them into the large cubicles right inside the doorway to the department. Then she marked the request with the cubicle number.

She carried the papers to the reception area. Normally, the college student Meredith would then contact the person who submitted the request and let him or her know from what cubby to pull the items. But, she had gone home for Thanksgiving break, so Calla slipped into the desk chair and sent several interoffice emails then went back to her stack of requests and started pulling files. By the time she felt like she'd made a dent in the work, Francine brought her several more requests. With just the two of them working in a department usually staffed by four, and at busy times, five or six, they worked quickly, not talking, just trying to stay on top of the requests. As the morning faded, they slowed down, giving them a chance to tackle the baskets of "to be filed" and the returned plans and specifications that had come in since the morning.

Slipping earbuds into her ears, she found an upbeat 80's music station on her phone and turned the volume up so that she could drown out the world and just file.

Ian leaned against the filing cabinet and watched Calla dance to the music pumping out of her earbuds. He could faintly hear it even from several feet away. It fascinated him how efficiently she worked while bopping her head around and shifting her shoulders to the rhythmic beat. He felt a silly grin cross his face while he waited for her to spin or turn and twist and see him, in a way hoping that it took a little bit longer so he could continue the sheer enjoyment of just watching her.

However, within seconds of that thought, she hit a file drawer with her hip to shut it, and turned and spotted him, halting mid-swing. She immediately stopped moving and yanked the earbuds out of her ears.

"You're really going to have to quit sneaking up on me like that," she mumbled, obviously embarrassed.

"Well, for one thing, I like what I see and," he watched her cheeks turn cherry red, "for another thing, I wasn't sneaking."

"You were sneaking. A little."

He laughed. "Maybe you shouldn't have your music so loud. How do you know when someone is here?"

She tapped the pocket of her pants. He could see the outline of her phone. "We normally have a receptionist, and she texts me." She looked at her watch. "Is it seriously 12:30? Wow, we've been so busy this morning that the time has flown by."

"Yes, and I only have about twenty minutes." With the Thanksgiving holiday this week, he had a last-minute meeting piled on top of a crisis meeting as people prepared to take a four-day holiday. "I just wanted to stop by and beg out of lunch. How about tomorrow?"

He could see the disappointment on her face and wondered why that filled him with some sort of male pride. "I would love that. Can I bring it?"

"I'm happy to take you out."

"You took me out last time. Yesterday. Remember? I'd like to think it's my turn."

Deciding not to argue, yet, he nodded. "Okay. Sounds good. I have to go. I'm very sorry. I'll see you tomorrow and make it up to you."

As he turned to leave, she said, "Where?"

Already thinking about the agenda for his upcoming meeting, he frowned when he looked back at her. "What?"

"See me where? Where do you want to meet? What time?"

"Ah, uh, coffee shop downstairs? Eleven-thirty? I'll check with Penny and confirm."

He turned away again and headed back to the elevator. As he stepped in, the phone in his hand vibrated. He answered it almost immediately. "Hi, Al."

"Hey. You coming to the one o'clock?"

He pressed the button for the seventh floor. "Yes. Headed to get my tablet now."

"I have Reubens from that place on Peachtree."

Wishing he could enjoy what Calla had packed this morning instead of corned beef and sauerkraut on rye, he nevertheless thanked him. "Sounds great. I'll grab cash when I go to my office, too."

"Get a couple bottles of water, too."

"Water, too, got it."

Five minutes later, they sat alone in the conference

room and bit into their sandwiches. Ian ate quickly, knowing that within ten minutes, the room would fill with people. "How was that dinner Saturday?" Al asked in-between bites. "With the flower girl?"

Ian contemplated the question as he chewed. "Tell you the truth? Incredible."

"And, did she properly thank you?"

Ian caught the tone of the question and answered the question Al didn't ask. "Not like that at all. The first time we even held hands was to bless the meal. She's something else."

"I see." Al grinned. "Do go on."

How much to elaborate? How did he explain to his best friend that he felt like he'd waited for someone like Calla Vaughn his entire life? "She's an amazing cook. She went to culinary school a few years ago. And, honestly, I feel like I'll never get tired of having conversations with her. She's bright, funny, kind of vivacious." He paused and caught Al staring at him with a huge grin on his face. "What?"

"Brother, I've known you since I was seventeen. I have never heard you talk like that about any girl, ever."

Ian set his sandwich down and wiped his buttery fingers on a paper napkin. "I never felt like this about any girl, ever. We had lunch yesterday after church, coffee this morning…" He picked up his water bottle and sat back in the conference room chair. "I've had a heck of a time concentrating today. All I want to do is go down to files and talk with her. Listen to her. Talk with her some more."

"Mmm hmm." Al nodded, rather knowingly. "I hear you. Can't wait to meet her myself."

"I bet you'll recognize her when you see her. You'll like her."

"Doesn't matter if I like her. She just has to pass the grandma test."

Ian's expression turned sharp. "That isn't funny."

"Oh, I know it's not funny," Al agreed. "It's not funny at all. I failed the grandma test. Remember?"

Ian opened his mouth to reply, but the conference door swung open and Brian, an architect in the firm, entered. "Smells like sauerkraut in here," he observed as he pushed a cart full of four-inch bound specifications for an upcoming central Alabama sports arena. As he reached the end of the table, he started placing a specifications book at each seat. "Those from that new place on Peachtree?"

Al nodded as he took his last bite. "They are."

"I hit them up last week. Man, I haven't had sandwiches that good since I left Miami."

"Word's getting out, too. Line was twenty minutes long today." He wrapped up his paper and balled it up. "Worth every minute."

"I hear you."

Ian finished his sandwich and pushed away from the table. "I need to check in with Penny. Be back by one." He stepped out through the door on the side of his office into the sea of cubicles and, thankfully, saw Penny at her desk. "Penny, am I free tomorrow at 11:30? My calendar looks good. I want to make sure there's been nothing last minute that hasn't propagated to me yet."

She pulled up the program on her computer and looked up at him. "Clear."

"Great. Schedule me in firm for lunch at 11:30. Unless Daddy Dixon appears, grab that half hour and growl. Okay?"

She smiled as if she knew he had lunch plans with Calla Vaughn tomorrow at eleven-thirty. "Sure. Where?"

"Coffee shop downstairs." He looked at his watch. "Have to get back to the meeting."

"You have a two-thirty after this one," she reminded him. He gave her a thumb's up as he went back to the conference room.

A s she pulled her bag out of her desk drawer, the phone at her elbow rang. Answering it almost absently, Calla checked in her bag to make sure she had the keys to lock the file room door. "File room, Calla Vaughn," she answered.

"Hello, Callie." At the sound of her stepmother, Becky Vaughn's voice mispronouncing her name, Calla's hands turned ice cold.

Trying to keep her voice from shaking, she demanded, "What do you want?"

"Oh, I'm just calling to let you know that if you were planning on coming home to daddy's house for Thanksgiving, I'll be in Cozumel. Jimmy, my boyfriend—you've met Jimmy, haven't you?—we're leaving tomorrow."

She'd met Jimmy. At her father's funeral. "Cozumel? Did Jimmy suddenly win the lottery?"

"No, silly. I got a new credit card last week. It's just dying for me to use it up. Ta!"

Becky didn't call her to keep her from coming "home" for Thanksgiving. She had no home. She'd sold that house before the headstone even came in for her father's grave. Becky called to make sure that Calla knew about another credit card in Calla's name.

Putting her head on her desk, a sob that she'd held back for far too long escaped her. No matter how hard she worked or how hard she tried, she would never get out of this pit. Her father's marriage to Becky had ruined her entire life, destroyed any possible good future. She just didn't realize the extent of it until after her father died.

After his funeral, Calla had taken a semester and a summer off from school, during which time Becky had gone through her father's savings in a matter of months. By the time it came time to pay her school bill, there was no money left. Calla tried to get a student loan, but apparently, she had tens of thousands of dollars of credit card debt, and the loan got declined.

That was when Calla discovered that Becky had used her name and social security number during her entire stint as step-mommy.

She'd never win. Another sob escaped and, with a wail, she let the tears fall. She ripped her glasses off her face and threw them on her desk. Anger made her ball her fists until her fingernails dug into her palms. She brought them up to her forehead violently, hitting herself so hard it nearly hurt. She pressed her fists hard into her head and battled the desire to break something, rip something, screech out loud.

"Calla?"

Startled, she whirled around in her chair, horrified to see Ian standing there. Immediately, she wiped her cheeks with both palms, wondering about the level of eye makeup leaving streaks along her cheeks. "Ian," she hiccuped. "I didn't hear you."

A confused frown marred his face. "Are you okay? What happened?"

She cleared her throat and stood quickly, grabbing her bag and the key to the door. "It's nothing. It's…" He pulled her to him and his arms came around her. She hadn't expected that, but without warning, she felt safer, freer, less like the world was closing in on her. "I'm sorry. I just fielded a phone call from my stepmother. She tends to have this kind of effect on me."

He shifted back so he could frame her wet face with his hands. "Is there something I can do?"

A joke about loaning her fifty-thousand dollars froze

on her tongue. Even in this overemotional state, she knew it wouldn't have gone over well. Instead, she shook her head. "I think I just need to build a bigger shell where she's concerned. Dad's been dead for three years. It shouldn't still hurt this bad."

She could see he didn't quite believe her but could tell when he decided not to push. He released her and stepped back far enough that she couldn't feel his body heat anymore. "I came down to see if you'd like a ride home? The weather is just as nasty as this morning."

Even though her knee-jerk answer would be to thank him and turn him down, she really wanted a ride home. "Thanks," she said, feeling calmer. "I would really like that. I appreciate you thinking about me."

They walked to the door together, and she pulled the double doors closed, locking them and setting the alarm. "What are you doing for Thanksgiving?" she asked.

"My family will all be at my grandmother's." He pressed the down button on the elevator. "You?"

"Sami invited me to dinner at her parents'. I'm making pies and veggies." They stepped into the empty elevator car, and Ian pressed the appropriate parking garage button. "Speaking of cooking, I'm looking forward to lunch tomorrow. I hope you like chili."

"That sounds wonderful, especially in this weather." She followed half a step behind him as they walked to his car, trying desperately to shake the emotional overload assaulting her right now from Becky's phone call.

He remotely unlocked the door to his car so that, by

the time they reached it, he could open her door for her.

As she settled into the seat and fastened her seatbelt, she wondered how to act with him. Part of her felt like she'd known him her whole life and should feel completely at ease. The other part of her knew they'd barely scratched the surface of what they could learn about each other and perhaps the almost kiss this morning was a little preemptive. Her mind went back and forth with all of the do's and don'ts and what's, and all of it swirled with the conversation she'd just had with Becky.

Ian opened the back door and set his backpack on the floorboard, then slid into the driver's seat. As he started the car, he rubbed his hands together. "Can't believe how fast the temperature dropped since this morning."

The safe conversation about weather gave her a little more time to shed all the negative emotions and find some balance again. "It should warm up again by next week. That's definitely one nice thing about living in the south—you only have to take tastes of fall and winter then everything goes back to right again."

He laughed. "Have you ever lived anywhere other than Atlanta?"

"No. Born and raised in the A-T-L. But, my dad came from Wisconsin. I spent many a white Christmas on the lake with my grandfather before he died. I don't think I'd enjoy living up there."

"I've always spent Christmas in Haiti, so I don't know about anything but mosquito nets and bags of tepid water."

"Bags? Not bottles?"

"Yeah. They come in bags, and you buy them in a big bag." He maneuvered his way out of the garage and turned in the direction of her apartment. For the next twenty minutes, they enjoyed easy conversation, remembering childhood Christmases and sharing stories. She told him about ice fishing, and he told her about bringing new soccer balls to a village. All too soon, he pulled into a spot near the front door and put the car in park, but did not turn off the engine.

"I'm sorry your stepmother hurt you so much," he said, shifting so he could partially face her. "If you need to talk about anything, let me know." He surprised her by reaching out and taking her hand. "No one should cause such an emotional reaction. Just know that you're not alone."

Her breath hitched, and she fought another surprising wave of emotion. "Thanks," she said, her voice hoarse. "I appreciate your concern, and I'm sorry that you saw me in such a state."

He raised an eyebrow. "Sorry? What does that mean?"

Her laugh sounded a little rough, despite its sincerity. "It means that right now, I still hope I look my best when you see me. I want my lipstick on and my hair straight. I changed clothes three times before church yesterday and twice before work this morning." She opened the door and grinned at him. "Ugly crying at my desk at six-fifteen on a Monday night does not constitute my best, and I'm truly sorry that happened."

He closed his eyes and gave a brief shake of his head. "Hey, Calla? For the record, I don't even understand what you just said."

"That's okay, Ian. You're a guy. There's no reason you would understand." She slid out of the car and leaned down to face him. "Thanks for the ride. I appreciate it more than you know."

Pulling her legs under her, Calla settled more comfortably on the couch with her notebook computer in her lap. The last pie for tomorrow's Thanksgiving dinner had just come out of the oven, and the fragrance of cinnamon and nutmeg mixed with Granny Smith apples wafted through the room, filling her with a feeling of comfort and happiness.

Since she didn't have to go into the office tomorrow, she could work as far into the night as she wanted. She had earbuds in her ears and typed as fast as her fingers could go, transcribing the video that played. She'd picked this one because as an instructor doing a voice-over for a presentation, he spoke clearly and concisely, and when he said words she didn't understand, most of the time they appeared on the screen. She barely had to pause.

An hour into the ninety-minute video when her cell phone chirped. Pausing the video, she picked it up and read the message from Sami.

SISTER'S WATER BROKE. HEADING UP TO CHARLOTTE WITH MY PARENTS. SORRY TO CANCEL THANKSGIVING! TALK SOON.

A smile crossed her face. She didn't think she'd ever met any sister more excited about a coming baby and wished she could go with her to Charlotte just to experience Sami meeting the baby for the first time.

Resuming her transcribing, she pressed play and started typing, then paused again. On an impulse, she picked up her phone and shot a quick text to Ian.

THANKSGIVING PLANS CANCELED. WANT TO COME BY FOR PIE TOMORROW EVENING? HATE TO SEE MY ALL MY WORK GO TO WASTE.

They'd enjoyed lunch together on Tuesday, but she hadn't seen him today. He had warned her of his full and busy schedule all day Wednesday. In fact, she hadn't even heard from him since the end of lunch today.

By the time she finished transcribing the video, formatted the captioning, and submitted it for billing, another two hours had gone by, and she still hadn't heard from him. Purposefully not letting that bother her, she went ahead and got ready for bed. She felt her energy draining from a long day at work and figured she could get up really early tomorrow in lieu of staying up late tonight.

When her alarm woke her at four on Thanksgiving morning, she saw a text from Ian time-stamped at two in the morning.

PICK YOU UP AT THREE. NOT TOO DRESSY.

A silly grin covered her face, and she held her phone to her chest as if she held a love letter. Did he truly plan to take her to his family Thanksgiving? Since no one could hear her, she went ahead and let the gleeful laugh out before texting him back.

I HAVE PIES AND SOME VEGGIES, TOO. DON'T FORGET.

Ten minutes later, she settled comfortably into the corner of her couch, a cup of coffee steaming at her elbow, the silly grin still on her face. As she accessed the site where she worked as a transcriber, she pulled up the list of available jobs. Seeing an upcoming episode of her favorite television show, she claimed it. While the video loaded in the interface, she put both of her hands on her cheeks and felt the smile. The sound of the opening credits pulled her out of her happy glow, and she paused the video to take a sip of coffee before getting to work.

A few minutes into transcribing, she got a new text.

PICK YOU AND THE PIES UP AT THREE. BREAD TOO? HOPE SO. SEE YOU THEN.

Ian entered the large house using his key. On the table that sat between the bottom steps of the double staircase sat a colossal vase of fall flowers lit by the ornate crystal chandelier. He walked across the gleaming tile, passed the leftmost staircase and through the door to his grandmother's sitting room.

He could see a low fire in the fireplace. That's where he found her, standing next to the marble mantle, looking at a picture of his parents. She had a very distant and wistful look on her face, and he cleared his throat before walking all the way over to her. As soon as she saw him, her eyes cleared and she smiled. He reached her and kissed both of her cheeks, breathing in the scent of roses that her lotions and sprays always smelled like.

"Grandmother," he greeted, "Happy Thanksgiving."

"Samuel," Annabelle Jones replied, patting the side of his arm, "you are early." She called him Ian until the day his father, her middle son, died. Then she began calling him Samuel, after his father.

"No, ma'am. I just stopped by to let you know I'm bringing a guest today."

"A guest?" Annabelle raised a perfectly plucked eyebrow. "And will this guest be a lady or a gentleman?"

He smiled, knowing she had immediately started praying that he planned to bring a guest of the romantic female persuasion, and not just a friend who found himself without a table this Thanksgiving. "A lady. Miss Calla Vaughn. I apologize for the last-minute invite, but she had her plans canceled late yesterday and has no family."

"No apologies necessary. You know my table is always open." She pursed her lips and looked him up and down. "You've never brought a young lady to our table before. I'd remember."

He threw his head back and laughed. "You'd remember, yes, ma'am." As he slipped his hands into his pockets, he thought back to the last five days, to the vibrant and fun woman with eyes as dark as the richest chocolates. "I've had one dinner, two lunches, and a coffee with her, grandmother. No wedding bells yet, please. I've only invited her because she found herself unexpectedly with nowhere else to go."

He cleared his throat and stopped himself from fidgeting. He knew he'd just spoken what amounted to a very small fib. Okay, a lie. He invited her because the text he read from her last night filled him with hopeful anticipation. He invited her because he couldn't stand the thought of not seeing her all day long. He invited her because he wanted to spend the day with her. "I like her, though. I do. She's really something. I hope you think so, too."

"Another first. Be still my heart." She walked over to a large arrangement of burgundy roses and picked a dying leaf off of a stem. "I won't make a big deal of it. Don't fret. Your old grandma-ma won't embarrass you today."

"You, dear lady, would have to try really hard to embarrass me in any way." He let a breath escape that he didn't realize he'd held. "I will warn you, though, you won't know her family. She's not exactly—"

The waving of her hand cut him off. "You assume too much about me. Always have. I disapprove of one girlfriend back in high school…"

When he realized that she didn't intend to finish the

sentence, he did it for her. "The one you embarrassed to the point of tears? After that, she wouldn't even look at me."

Annabelle sat on her flowered settee and patted the cushion next to her. "You obviously don't have a clue what happened. That girl, I don't remember her name—"

"Melissa Posner." He pictured the athletic blonde who led the cheerleading squad. "Missy."

"Okay, Missy." She cleared her throat and straightened the gold watch on her wrist. "I walked in on her talking to the maid Bea in such a tone that I couldn't believe a teenager was speaking. I was appalled. So, I tested her, and she failed." Her hazel eyes met his, and he could see no regret in them. "I know that was the last time you brought someone home. But, it had nothing to do with my snobbery and everything to do with not wanting you to end up with a woman like her."

He tried to remember the incident, the exact words that his grandmother had spoken, anything at all, but so much time had passed, and he couldn't grab all of the details from his very hazy memory. "I've always resisted bringing anyone else home because I assumed you wouldn't approve, that's true. I wish you'd said something to me before."

"There was no need before." She patted his hand. "Now, if you have someone you feel would survive my scrutiny, however mistaken that thought is, this must be someone incredibly special. Because, I imagine if she weren't, you would have simply made plans with her after coming here or something of the sort. Bringing her here, with your uncles and me, now, tells me that she is someone I need to pay attention to."

Ian closed his eyes then demanded, "What about Al, Grandma?"

His grandmother froze. She turned slowly and met his eyes. "Samuel, that is between your sister and me. I understand you may feel protective of your sister and your best friend, but you do not know the details, and I will not gossip. So, I would appreciate your trust in this matter, and I will thank you if you never bring that subject up with me again in the future."

Ian tasted copper on his tongue. He swallowed and said. "All right, Grandma. But it doesn't make me feel better about bringing my friend over for Thanksgiving dinner."

She crossed her arms, then said, "Then perhaps you should tell me about her, Samuel."

His mind drifted to Calla and pictured her hitting the filing cabinet drawer with her hip. A silly smile crossed his face at the image. "She loves Jesus. And she's really fun to be around. I think you'll like her." He looked at his watch. "I have to go. She is bringing food, by the way."

She frowned. "Food?" She said the word as if it felt foreign to her tongue. "I'm not sure I understand."

"Trained chef, grandmother. Trust me. You'll be happy."

"What kind of food?"

"Pies." He smiled and winked. "And some kind of

vegetable."

"I have a caterer, Samuel. Our Thanksgiving dinner table is not some country tent meeting potluck." Again, she said the word potluck as if pronouncing a foreign phrase attached to an equally foreign concept.

He loved his grandmother. She'd sell her family jewelry if it meant helping someone in need. She could also don the upper-crust snob mantle whenever she felt the need. "I understand. But, like I said, trained chef. You asked me to trust you? Trust me. You'll be happy. And," he said in a slightly warning tone, "you'll be thankful because I'm saying please."

The sigh she heaved gave the impression that she just conceded a hard-fought battle. "Very well. Go into the kitchen and get the appropriate dishes for your lady friend. My table will be set with matching dinnerware, even if it's put together hodgepodge."

"Hardly fair, grandmother," Ian said with a smile as he leaned forward to kiss her cheek. "I'll see you in a few hours."

CHAPTER 6

C alla stared at the reflection of her third wardrobe change in the mirror and smoothed down the sides of her dark green jacket. She wore a suede skirt the color of rich caramel, dark brown boots, and a scarf that pulled all the colors together. As she examined her outfit, she worried that she had overdressed. He did say not too dressy in his text, right? Was this too dressy? What if everyone there wore blue jeans and football jerseys?

Before she could change outfits yet again, her doorbell rang. This outfit would have to do, she thought, as she rushed through her apartment and opened the door. She smiled when she saw Ian in a dark blue button-down shirt and a pair of khaki pants. Perfect. She hadn't overdressed.

"Hi there," she greeted with a grin, stepping forward to hug him. "I'm ready. I just need to grab the food."

He brushed his lips over her cheek as he hugged her back, then stepped fully into the apartment. She gestured at the serving dish in his hand. "What's that?"

He cleared his throat. "My grandmother is sort of set in her ways. She doesn't like a mismatched table. She sent me with a serving dish for your vegetables." He held it out. "I feel like I should preface that with an apology."

"Nonsense." She took the dish and went into the kitchen, pulling the pan of roasted Brussels sprouts and butternut squash out of the oven. "It makes perfect sense. Appearance is actually a huge part of dining."

Ian walked over to the counter where she had an apple pie and a pecan pie. He leaned down and sniffed the apple pie. She'd sliced Granny Smith apples and arranged them in a pattern to look like a rose in full bloom. She'd scalloped the crust so that it looked like the edge of a lace doily. Over the top of the fruit, she'd sprinkled cinnamon, a sauce made from brown sugar and butter, and then grated fresh nutmeg. "This looks incredible," he remarked, smelling the rosette pie again. "Apple pie is my favorite."

"If I'd known that, I would have made two," Calla

said, and immediately felt her cheeks heat. Where did such a flirtatious comment come from?

"The way to a man's heart," he teased as she packed the pies into the portable carrier, carefully not damaging the crust she had painstakingly designed.

"That's the rumor." She scooped the vegetables into the casserole dish and pulled the box of plastic wrap out of the drawer. "I have an arsenal if that's the case. You might consider yourself warned."

She moved around the kitchen with a grace and poise that looked different from her movements in the file room. Her movements there looked improvised. Here she looked contained, practiced, disciplined, and smooth. She moved with confidence and mastery. He felt like he was watching a professional ice skater or prima ballerina. The entire time she arranged the food, she continued talking about food though she captured his eyes and his heart more than his ears.

"You know how in the Bible it talks about how Eve saw that the apple was pleasing to the eye? Isn't that interesting? Even the first people on earth desired food that looked good. You know?"

"I think *you* look good," Ian said.

"What?"

Ian grinned. "I said I think you look good, Calla Vaughn. Beautiful, even."

Calla leaned against her counter, pausing in her practiced movements long enough to blush and grin. "Well, I'm not food, Mr. Jones."

Ian shook his head. "No, ma'am." He smiled as he stared into her eyes. "You are not food. You are something else."

She broke eye contact first, turning back to care for her vegetables. Quietly, she said, "Thank you, Ian."

"Tell me something, Calla Vaughn."

"What would you like to know, Ian Jones?"

"Why did you leave culinary school?"

The question threw her off, and she momentarily lost her poise. She found her hands fumbling on the plastic wrap, tangling it and making it rip. With her back to him, she closed her eyes, breathed deeply through her nose, then carefully covered the casserole dish with a sheet of plastic, this time very smooth and perfect.

Knowing she smiled an overly bright smile, but unable to do anything about it, she turned to him and said, "That's a long story. Can we talk about it later, when I'm not a nervous wreck on my way to your family's house?"

He stared at her with serious eyes for several seconds before finally nodding. "Sure." He cleared his throat. "I'm not trying to be nosy. I just want to get to know you better."

With an uncommon boldness, she stepped toward him. "Here's something about me you don't know, but that Sami and Penny and probably half a dozen other assistants know about me. I've had somewhat of a schoolgirl crush on you since I started working at Dixon Contracting. That's three years. The reason I know

Penny so well is that if it was for you, I did it first and foremost, and she started noticing. It feels really weird to say it out loud, especially to you, but it's the truth. I didn't tell you about the flowers the first night because you accepted my dinner invitation, and being able to cook for you was like a dream come true."

Suddenly very uncomfortable and self-conscious, she picked up the serving dish and started out of the kitchen. "I'm ready to go if you can grab that pie container."

"Hey," he said, stopping her as she walked past him. When she turned to ask him what, he took the dish from her hands and set it on the counter next to him before he cupped her face with his hands. He looked into her eyes for several seconds before he slipped the glasses off of her face and lowered his lips to hers. The smell of his aftershave overwhelmed her as his soft, warm lips covered hers. She hesitated only a second before sliding her hand along his smooth cheek and stepping just a little closer, rising up on her toes to get that much nearer to him. It lasted just long enough to have her catching her breath, then he lifted his head and took half a step back.

"Thanks for making apple pie." His voice was deep, hoarse.

Clearing her throat and trying to do the mental shift back to pie, she took her glasses from him and straightened her jacket. Somehow, she managed to get her brain to form a response, and then communicate with her mouth - the same mouth still tingling from the kiss. "Glad I didn't like the look of the pumpkins at the market."

An hour later, Calla observed the dynamics of his family at the table. Ian's grandmother, Annabelle, sat at the head of the table, with Ian to her left. Calla sat between him and Ian's sister, Heidi. Ian's uncle Dwayne sat at the foot of the table, with his wife Beth to his left. To finish off the circle, his other uncle Theodore and his wife Donna, who sat to Annabelle's right. Over hors-d'oeuvres, Annabelle had explained to Calla that the children, all of Ian's cousins, spent Thanksgiving with their in-laws every year so the entire family could be together for their annual Christmas mission trip to Haiti.

Ian's sister, an engineer who designed roadways for the city of Atlanta, had dark brown hair and hazel eyes that seemed to shift between green and brown. Calla really enjoyed talking to her.

They chatted comfortably, like old friends. The anxiety Calla had felt about what awaited her at this dinner faded with every passing moment. Despite the luxurious surroundings in the old plantation mansion and the presence of a uniformed staff, every family member treated her in a manner that she found very welcoming and kind. In no time, she felt like they had enfolded her into the family.

"You met Ian at work?" Heidi asked.

"Yes. He had to push my car out of the way in the parking garage," Calla said, laughing. "It hasn't been hard to find the silver lining in that cloud."

Ian took a swallow of his water and leaned over Calla to speak to his sister. "It was really over a misdelivered flower arrangement. She sent flowers to her friend, Sami, to thank her for helping her with the car. But the florist delivered them to me since father insisted I be called Samuel instead of Ian. So, I guess there's a silver lining to that as well." Everyone laughed, and Ian took Calla's hand under the table. He gave her palm a gentle and reassuring squeeze, either to convey support or just because he needed to have that momentary contact with her, she didn't know. All she knew was that she liked it and missed his touch as soon as he let go of her hand.

Ian sat next to Calla and watched her interact with his family, listening to stories he'd heard a dozen times in his lifetime. He laughed at the appropriate times, interjected when things got a little exaggerated, and generally enjoyed every single moment of this Thanksgiving more than he thought he'd ever enjoyed the holiday before.

Calla was fun and had a good sense of humor, and a laugh that brought a smile to his lips. She charmed his uncles, made friends with his sister and his aunts, and he could tell she impressed his grandmother. He loved the fact that the dish that had held her roasted vegetables left the table empty, and that the beautiful works of art she created in her pies caused compliments to come from all parts of the table.

He tried to remind himself that he had only officially met Calla less than a week ago and that these kinds of feelings didn't just appear out of nowhere. The more his mind tried to tell his heart that, the less his heart listened or believed. Ian felt something special about his attraction for her. He could only hope and pray that she felt the same way.

As the maid served the pie, he put an arm around the back of her chair and leaned toward her. She finished saying something to Heidi and turned toward him, half a smile on her lips. It took considerable restraint to keep from kissing her then and there in front of God and everyone, but she must have read his mind because the smile slowly faded and she glanced at his lips.

Her voice touched his ears like a gentle caress. "You know what I'm most thankful for today, Ian?"

"What's that, Calla?"

"I'm so thankful you invited me today," she said very softly, her words only for his ears, only for him.

He reached out and took the hand she'd set in her lap. "And I am very thankful you agreed to come. You have certainly brightened up this table."

"Which pie, Mr. Samuel?" the maid at his elbow asked.

He straightened and let go of Calla's hand. "Apple, if you please, Velma. And bring another slice after everyone else is served. Thank you so much." On top of the pie sat a perfectly formed football shaped quenelle of cinnamon ice cream. It had started to melt and dribbled down the sides of the pie in a perfect formation. His mouth watered at the sight of it as he picked up his fork.

At the first bite, the tartness of apples warred with the sweetness of the caramel sauce, accentuated by the spices and his tongue could barely keep up with the amazing experience of the taste. He closed his eyes and slowly chewed, wanting to savor every bite.

After dessert, Annabelle stood up and addressed the family. "This has been a delightful meal," she said with a smile. "It is always a treasure to have all my children available to me. I am especially happy that Ian brought a guest because I have tremendously enjoyed getting to know her and I'm sure I've not had vegetables that well prepared in a very long time." She looked at Ian with a mischievous smile. "We won't tell her this is the first time you've ever brought a girl home to dinner." Ian barked out a laugh and glanced at Calla, who looked surprised. He took her hand and laced his fingers through hers, enjoying the feel of her smooth skin against his.

"With sincere thankfulness," his grandmother continued, "I pray for each of you daily, and hope that you have a beautiful holiday season. Now, regarding Haiti. If you are filling a container for me to ship ahead of our trip this year, I have a list at the front table in the hall for you to use as your guide for supplies. After the hurricanes this year, I know that one vital need is powdered milk." She stepped away from the table and pushed her chair in. "You are now released from your family obligation," she said with a smile, making the whole table laugh, "and I love you all."

As everyone got up from the table, Ian led Calla to his grandmother's sitting room. They found Annabelle sitting next to Dwayne with a tablet in her lap, discussing packing lists. "I've already sent the money, ready to pay the customs officials' extortion," Dwayne said. "The containers should get there about a week before you do. I have a team of Haitian workers who are already contracted to unload the containers and truck them up the mountain."

"Perfect," Annabelle said, "Are you sure you sent enough?"

"With the hurricanes this year, we're thinking the extortion won't be so bad. But, yes, we're sure we sent enough."

Ian glanced at Calla and saw the confusion on her face. "Usually, containers filled with things like building materials require a bribe to get through customs. The extortion is almost a standard operating procedure." He looked back at his grandmother. "Calla and I are going to head out, grandma."

She stood in a fluid motion and hugged him. He breathed in the smell of roses that lingered even after she stepped over to Calla. "It was such a pleasure to meet you. I hope to see you again."

Calla smiled and didn't hesitate to hug Annabelle. "It was wonderful. Thank you so much for inviting me."

"You are welcome any time."

As they stepped outside into the dusk, Ian took Calla's hand and led her along the circular driveway. "You certainly made an impression," he said quietly, stopping at his car to open the passenger's door for her.

When he settled into the driver's seat, she looked

over at him and surprised him by asking, "If you've never brought a girl home, how do you know that's not how they would treat any female guest of yours?"

He could see her grin in the dim light and grinned back. "Despite orphanages and mission's trips, there's still a very superior air about my family. I can assure you that if you had not passed muster, so to speak, you would have very much realized it."

After a moment of silence, she said, "I'm just glad they liked my food."

Surprised, he asked, "What do you mean? Of course, they liked your food."

He saw her slight shrug. "I'm afraid that's part of the creative brain. I'm riddled with insecurities about my food. Every time. I wonder why I even cook until someone eats something and they love it so much. Then I get filled with creative energy and can't wait until I get to cook again."

"That sounds absolutely exhausting."

She laughed. "Why do you think I'm tired all the time?"

He found that he rather liked her brain. They enjoyed comfortable conversation all the way back to her apartment. When he walked to the door, he leaned down and brushed his lips against her cheek. "Let me know when you're feeling up to making another apple pie," he teased.

Despite his intentional teasing tone, she said, "How about Sunday? After church?"

Knowing he had the whole weekend free, he nodded. "I can do that."

"Perfect." She unlocked her door then turned back to face him. "I very much look forward to it." After staring up at him with eyes that looked very nearly black in the dim corridor light, she softly said, "Goodnight, Ian."

He closed his eyes and took a deep breath through his nose. Then he opened his eyes, turned, and purposefully put one foot in front of the other all the way down the corridor to his car.

Calla sat in Ian's desk chair and pulled her legs up underneath her. She'd worn a long skirt today so she could wear long underwear underneath it. The temperature had chilled this week before Christmas, and the morning walk to the train station in thirty-three degrees made her thankful for warm boots and foresight. She blew on the surface of the hot cup of coffee in her hand and watched her breath create ripples in the dark liquid.

Ian perched on the chair in front of his drafting table, his eyes narrowing as he looked at a set of plans and spoke to the contractor on the phone. She enjoyed watching him when he worked, admired the intensity of his concentration. She didn't feel a need to interject, to remind him of her presence, to try to get his attention. No, she just wanted to watch him, watch the expressions cross his face, watch his brain work through whatever problem the person on the other end of the line had presented to him.

He hung up the phone and made several notations on a notepad in front of him before looking at her. His face gradually softened as his eyes focused on her. "Sorry about that."

"No reason to be sorry," she claimed, straightening her legs and sitting properly in the chair. "Your work day starts way earlier than mine."

"Yeah, I have to get to it, really."

"I understand." She held up the coffee cup. "I'm taking this with me."

"Please do." His phone chirped with a text, and she stood, grabbing her coat and her bag. He had the phone to his ear when she started to walk by him, but he grabbed her arm and pulled her to him for a very quiet, brief kiss. When she pulled away, he winked at her, then his eyes grew serious again, and he started talking on the phone.

As she slipped out of his office and closed the door behind her, she paused at Penny's desk. "Any big plans for Christmas?" Penny asked, cutting her eyes to Ian's door then back at Calla with a mischievous grin.

Calla smiled and settled into the chair next to Penny's desk. She spoke in a quiet tone, not wanting to have any of the other assistants or interns in the cubicle area overhear. "Yesterday, he told me that his cousin couldn't go to Haiti this year. So, he asked if I wanted to go since the plane ticket was already bought."

"Haiti is hardly a romantic getaway," Penny said. "You should push for Cancun or something."

Calla cheeks flooded with color. "It's not intended to be a romantic getaway. It's supposed to be a mission trip."

"Nevertheless." Her phone sounded a tone, and immediately Calla heard Ian's voice coming through the speaker. "Penny, I need you."

"Yes, sir." As Penny stood, she leaned down toward Calla and whispered, "Seriously, he could take you anywhere."

Calla understood that she and Penny had a different moral compass, especially when it came to men and relationships...and relationship boundaries. Instead of arguing purity over temptation, she just smiled and said, "Penny, anywhere on earth would feel romantic with him. Have a great day."

A few minutes later, she sat at Sami's desk. Sami gave her a half grin. "Haiti, huh?"

"It's an annual Christmas tradition." She thought of the news footage she'd seen of the island country when she'd transcribed a news report. "It was pretty much destroyed when that big hurricane hit it in September."

"I know. I remember." She took a sip of her tea. "Seems kind of soon to be asking you out on a trip out of the country, though."

"One month." Calla sat back and held her mug with both hands. She couldn't remember a time when she didn't spend time with Ian on a daily basis. She smiled and thought back to the very first time she opened her apartment door to him. "Only one month? How is that possible?"

"Works that way sometimes," Sami said. She blinked, and Calla could see the gold glitter of her eyeshadow - the same gold that matched the ornaments painted with glittery fabric paint on her dark green dress. She'd obviously worn it for the evening's annual Dixon Contracting Christmas party. "You've never been more relaxed, though, honestly. I think it's great." Calla glanced at her watch as Sami fielded a call. She had another five minutes before she had to head down to the file room. When Sami hung up, she asked, "Have you told Ian about your stepmom?"

Instantly, her stomach knotted painfully. She pressed her lips together and slowly shook her head. "No. Not yet."

"Calla," Sami chided.

"How do I, even?"

Sami leaned forward as if someone could overhear them. "Calla, you have to tell him. He has to know the mess that woman created before he develops any deeper feelings for you. Keeping it from him is not fair to him."

She was right. She knew it. She sighed. "I know. I'm just so afraid that I'll lose him."

Sami narrowed her eyes. "I hear you. But, better now than a month from now, or a year. You two, you're like this perfection in a couple. Even Al Carpenter thinks so, and he's super defensive about Ian."

Calla sighed. "I think I've decided to press formal charges."

Sami, who had spent years trying to convince Calla to do just that widened her eyes in surprise. "Shut up. Really?"

Thinking about Ian, how ordered and careful he kept his life, and how chaotic and out of control hers had become, she nodded. "I think it's the right thing to do. And, I think it will be easier to tell him about it when I've done exactly what I should have done three years ago."

"Good for you." Sami leaned forward. "But, this is something that the longer you go without saying something, the more it's going to seem like deceit. You don't want that."

She didn't want that. Hours later, in her sea of filing cabinets and drawers, she resolved to tell Ian about it. After Christmas. After she filed charges.

CHAPTER 7

Ian sat next to a dozing Calla as the jet airplane entered Atlanta airspace. He leaned forward and looked out the window, analyzing the last two weeks. He'd spent the first week in Ti Peligre helping with the rebuilding of a footbridge over the Thomonde River that the hurricane in September had wiped out. When Calla arrived on Christmas Eve, he'd met her at the airport in Port-au-Prince. They spent the night on two-inch mattresses covered by mosquito netting on the flat roof of a church, which provided a refreshing respite from the tropical heat. The next morning, they had driven two hours to Cariesse to catch the ferry to Anse-à-Galets on La Gonâve Island.

Emmanuel Danos, a Haitian neighbor of the orphanage and the fiancé of his cousin, Hettie, had met them at the ferry in a small four-wheel drive all-terrain vehicle. They proceeded to drive for hours on the worn paths of lava rock the locals referred to as roads through narrow passages of rough terrain up the mountain to the village of Ti Palmiste. Finally, they arrived at the orphanage his family's mission ran.

The first time he'd taken this journey, his mother had carried him as a six-month-old in a sling made out of a large sheet of cloth fastened with a ring, allowing her to hold him hands-free while she worked and walked. By contrast, as he experienced everything with Calla, he felt like he experienced it for the first time in his life. The excitement, wonder, fear, and exhaustion that she felt radiated from her, and he felt all of those things, too. It breathed new life into something that had at some point become rote to him. Seeing the mission through her eyes made him seek to serve God on this trip with a renewed heart and spirit. It deepened his prayer life in a way he couldn't begin to have fathomed. It excited him and made him want to tell her everything about this island, its people, the language.

When his grandmother had met them at the gates of the orphanage, she'd hugged Calla enthusiastically. For the next three days, they'd worked nonstop, rebuilding a fence that had blown down, fixing a wall and roof at the school that had collapsed under a falling palm tree, and shopping for chickens and goats at the marketplace to replace those that disappeared in the storm.

He'd watched her interact with the children, had observed the sheer joy on her face when she watched them open their Christmas presents his grandmother had brought. He watched the sorrow overtake her as they tried on shoes and socks and accepted them with the same enthusiasm an American child would show for a new laptop or smartphone. She'd sat for hours while a teenager had braided her hair, playing marbles with some younger kids the whole time. And then, in the daylight hours, watched her work until her palms bled.

She cried when they left. He had a feeling that some part of her considered staying there permanently. The way the children responded to her, he knew his cousin who lived there full-time wouldn't have hesitated to bring her on as a member of the staff.

Unfortunately, Calla had limited time available to take off from work, so he left early with her, leaving his family behind so he could accompany her home. Retracing their steps, they went back down the mountain to the ferry, back to spend the night on the roof of the church, then to catch an early flight back to Atlanta. As they boarded the plane in Port-au-Prince, he wanted to warn her about reintegration and the hard time she could have reconciling the American way of life with what she left behind. He knew from experience, though, that no words would or could explain the pain and heartbreak she would feel. She would have to go through it, and she would know next time how to begin to steel her heart against the culture shock she'll feel just getting off the plane.

For now, though, she rested with her braided head on his shoulder and her hand in his. He wondered how something as simple as her holding his hand could possibly feel so right. He'd known for days now that he had fallen very deeply in love with her. But, they'd had that first dinner just six weeks ago. Hardly enough time for such declarations or talk of a future. Best to wait. Give her time.

As he looked out the window and watched the pavement rise up to meet the plane, then felt the pull of force as his body tried to keep going forward when the pilot applied the brakes, she sat up. He watched her as she slipped her glasses on and ran her palms over the braids in her hair before she looked at him. When her eyes met his, he felt a rush of emotion, and it took all his willpower to keep from saying the words out loud. Instead, he just cupped her face with his palm and leaned forward to give her a slow kiss as the plane came to a stop at the gate.

"Thanks for coming this week," he said as they stood and pulled bags out of the overhead compartment.

"I feel like coming back was the wrong thing to do," she admitted, putting the strap of her bag over her head so that the bag crossed her body. She started inching forward out of the plane. "I feel like I left a part of me back there in Haiti."

"Imagine how it is for my family. We do Haiti every Christmas, and then an orphanage in Ecuador every summer. I keep waiting for my grandmother to announce she's taking up permanent residence at one or the other. I think the fundraising she regularly does for the missions is what keeps her here."

She stood in front of him, and he fingered one of her dark braids. "I could get used to this look," he said, remembering the way she'd just sat and let the girls minister to her.

She put a hand on her head almost self-consciously. "When I looked in the mirror in the airport restroom back in Haiti, I didn't really recognize myself," she said with a smile. "It took so long to put in that I'm loathe to take them out. But I will soon. They're already looking a little messy."

"They'll be fine for a couple more days. I'll help you take them out if you want."

He watched her cheeks fuse with color before she looked up at him with surprise in her eyes. He immediately wanted to know what thought had crossed her mind, but didn't ask. She just said, "Thank you, Ian," very quietly.

In no time they strolled up the jetway toward the red-coated stewards directing the passengers toward US Customs. They held hands naturally, like they'd done it all their lives. They chose a line and, in a way, Ian wanted to pick the longest one. He knew real life would pick back up again on the other side of that checkpoint. Work, church obligations, more work—things that would keep them apart for good chunks of the time.

When they got to the front of the line, Calla went

forward first. She handed her passport to the Customs agent. From his place several feet away, Ian watched Calla's frown as the agent stood up from his chair. Calla looked over at Ian with a worried expression on her face, but when he stepped forward, the agent held a hand out, palm up.

"Stay right there, sir."

Seconds later, two uniformed security agents approached. One took Calla by her arm and led her away. The other retrieved her bag and accepted her passport from the Customs agent. She looked over her shoulder at Ian, but the guard kept propelling her forward relentlessly.

Ian rushed to the Customs agent. "What's going on? Where are they taking her?" he demanded.

"Sir? Calm down. Hand me your passport, please," the agent directed, looking at him with measuring eyes.

As he handed over his passport and his declaration form, Ian pleaded with him. "Please. What's going on?"

The agent looked over his shoulder as a door closed behind Calla and her armed escort. Then he looked back at Ian and said, "Her passport was flagged. There was an arrest warrant for her. That's all I can tell you." He looked down at the passport and back at Ian and began the brief interview to allow him back into the country. "What was the purpose of your trip to Haiti?"

Calla sat in the cold metal chair at a dark gray metal table in a room with no color and bad lighting. Scuff marks from countless shoes broke up the monotony of the dull green floor. A mirror reflected the gray room back at her, and she wondered who, if anyone, stood on the other side watching her. A chill in the air made her want to rub her arms, but she didn't want to look defensive. She'd planned on changing clothes at the airport, and her thin cotton dress worn for the tropical climate of Haiti did little to shield her from the cold chair or the cold air.

Where was Ian? What could he possibly think of her now? All the happy, comforting, familiar relationship she'd felt until now had probably dissolved the second the officer put the handcuffs on her in the interview room outside the Customs area.

She stared at the detective sitting in front of her. He had dark hair and olive skin but spoke with a southern Georgia accent. "Miss Vaughn," he drawled, "let's go over this one more time."

Calla sat back in the metal chair and tried to not look as scared as she felt. "Sir, I don't know what else you want me to say. I know that my father's widow did this. But I don't know where she is. She called me right before Thanksgiving and said she was going to Mexico."

"Right. Mexico. That's what you said. What I'm trying to understand is that if you dislike her as much as you clearly do, why would you have let this go on for as long as you have?"

Calla took a deep breath and slowly let it out of her

mouth. "I've asked myself that a hundred times a day for three years. I..." she felt her throat constricting, and she paused long enough to clear her throat and fight back tears. "I think originally it was grief over my father's death. And then, I don't know, it was almost a sense of disbelief like, surely, I was wrong about everything I was finding out. At some point, I think I adopted a victim mentality. I felt like a victim, I thought like a victim. She used it. She used me. She lorded it over me like she knew exactly how I felt and thought. And I just took it. Like some whipped dog. Does that make sense?"

He inclined his head as if to agree with her, but his lips pursed and he said, "I just don't understand, Miss Vaughn, how anyone can allow another person to put them in debt close to $60,000. And that's not even counting another $10,000 in bad checks from last week. So, I'm just trying to understand how you let this happen, and really trying to ascertain how complicit you were in the entire thing."

"I wasn't!" She slapped her hand on the table so hard the sound echoed around the room. Her voice stayed raised. "I had nothing to do with it. She started when I was fourteen years old. I live in a one-room apartment, I don't own a car, I work two jobs, and more than half of all of my income goes to service debt that she made in my name, and I have nothing. Nothing!" She took her glasses off and rubbed her eyes. "I had planned to talk to the police about her tomorrow. Seriously. I talked to my friend Sami about it before I went on my mission's trip."

He turned a page in the open file folder. "We have no record of her going to Mexico. Where would she have gone?"

"Sir," her voice sounded tired, ragged, hoarse. "I have no idea. I really don't. I don't know anything about her. I don't even know if the man that's with her is actually named Jimmy."

"Do you have an address for her?"

He'd asked these questions four other times. "I haven't seen her since the day of my father's funeral. The funeral she attended on Jimmy's arm. The funeral where she laughed about his death and sent everyone home." She hadn't said any of that out loud before, and that caused the detective to raise an eyebrow.

She wearily rubbed the back of her neck. "She called me right before Thanksgiving. She called my work extension. I can tell you the day. Maybe you can get a phone number from the phone records."

A knock on the door interrupted them. The uniformed police officer standing by the door opened it, and a youngish woman in a blue business suit walked in. She had brown hair cut to her chin and striking green eyes. "Hello. I'm Miss Vaughn's attorney. I'd like a moment with my client please," she said to the detective. He looked at her for several seconds before shutting the file folder in front of him and getting up. The men left without another word. As soon as the door shut behind him and the officer, the woman spoke to Calla as she pulled a yellow legal pad out of her bag and sat down in the metal chair across from her. "My name is Mary Ann. Sam—," she paused and corrected herself, "Ian is my cousin. He called me."

Hot tears filled her eyes for the first time since the Customs agent took her passport from her. "I don't—"

Mary Ann reached over and took her hand. "Don't worry. Okay? I need to know what's going on so I can know what we need to do. Ian didn't have any information for me."

Calla took a deep, shaky breath. "When I was fourteen, my father's wife used my identity for the first time. That was almost ten years ago. In that time, she has put me into almost $60,000 in debt. This arrest was for $10,000 in bad checks that she's written in the last couple of weeks. The checking account was in my name and was a closed account. The police think we're in cahoots."

Mary Ann rapidly made notes on her yellow legal pad. "Okay," she said. "Have you ever pressed charges? Filed a civil suit? Reported her to law enforcement at any time?"

Calla shook her head.

"Why have you not pressed charges against your stepmother? Is it because your father doesn't want you to?"

"My father died when I was twenty. But, I don't think he ever knew anything about any of it. I think she's a con artist and I think that my father was her victim. What do they call it? Her mark?"

"If that's the case, why have you never even once gone to the police?"

With a sigh, Calla answered, "I don't know. I'm sure

a psychiatrist would have a field day analyzing my psyche right now. But I'll honestly tell you that my relationship with Ian made me realize that going to the police was exactly what I needed to do and I planned to go this week."

Marianne made notes. For several minutes, the sound of the scratch of her pen on the paper resonated in the otherwise silent room. Finally, she nodded. "Okay. Don't say another word unless I'm in the room with you. I'll get you out of here, and we'll talk some more."

"That's it? Will this go away?"

Marianne shut the lid to her pen and laced her fingers together, resting her hands on top of her notepad. "I think that, eventually, we can prove you were not complicit. As long as you're not hiding material merchandise or something like that. No expensive trips or lifestyle. I think if we can find out if the stepmother has a past, maybe charges pending in another state or something, it will go further toward proving your innocence. Your lack of pursuing legal matters might have something to do with your stepmother being someone in authority, and then you having a victim mindset. It's hard to say what the D.A. will accept as fact. But we'll give him everything and then see what happens. I know him. He's fair, and he's not going to pursue charges if there's nothing substantial there."

Tears poured out of Calla's eyes. "I can't pay you."

Marianne reached over and covered her hand with her own. "Actually, we can work it out but that's something we'll worry about much later. One thing at a time." She stood up and said, "Right now. I'll go up and see about getting you released."

CHAPTER 8

I an sat with his back to the arm of the couch and looked at Calla. In the two weeks since he'd seen her last, she'd taken the braids out of her hair and the tan she'd gotten while in Haiti had faded. She had dark circles under her eyes, and her cheeks looked sallow, as if she had lost weight.

He'd come here because Al thought talking to her face-to-face would help him. But, as he stared at her, he found himself growing angry as the hurt tried to infiltrate his heart again.

She'd let him in then sat on the other end of the couch, legs pulled up to her chest, tears sliding down her cheeks. It took a lot not to reach out to her and try to comfort her. He reminded himself of the two weeks of silence and unanswered texts and phone calls.

She didn't speak, so he finally broke the silence. "At what point were you going to tell me what was going on with you?"

Calla rested her temple against her knees as she turned her head to look at him. "I'd promised myself after Christmas. I wanted to press charges against her before I told you about it. Plus, I had a feeling you wouldn't want to be with me anymore, and I didn't want to spoil your holiday."

He took a deep breath through his nose and slowly closed his eyes. "Well, having you arrested at the airport was probably better than just telling me the truth. I can see that."

The sound of her breath hitching made him open his eyes again. "Obviously, I didn't know…"

"Right. Because if there was a chance you might be arrested upon your return to American soil, why you might have just considered staying in Haiti? Like you told me you wanted to do?" He surged to his feet and walked across the carpet, feeling like a caged animal in the small room. "I asked you, Calla, flat-out why you quit culinary school. That first week of our relationship, I gave you an opportunity to be honest with me."

"On our way to your family's Thanksgiving dinner!" She ripped her glasses off her face and threw them on the coffee table, then dug her palms into her eyes. "How am I supposed to start that conversation, huh? 'Sorry, Ian. You probably don't want to continue to see me because my stepmother is a con artist—wanted in three states it turns out—and she has destroyed my name and credit to the tune of tens of thousands of dollars.' Yeah, you would have helped me pack up those pies and taken me right on over to grandma's house."

Rage burned behind his eyes and he spoke without thinking. "So, you just bring me in deeper, make me fall in love with you, and then what? I bail you out? Write a big fat check, and you're in the clear? Taking your cues from your stepmom now?"

As soon as he spoke the words, he knew he didn't believe them. He opened his mouth to retract them, but Calla gasped and surged to her feet. "Get out!" She raced across the room and threw the deadbolt on her door. "Get out of my house. Get out of my life."

Immediately, the rage dissipated, like air from a balloon. His shoulders slumped forward. "I'm sorry, Calla. That was—"

"That was exactly what you think of me. Get out. Leave. Just go. I'll find another job, so you don't have to worry about running into me anymore."

She opened the door and crossed her arms over her chest. For the first time since he walked into her apartment, no tears fell from her eyes. Resigned, he walked to the door but stopped in front of her. "Calla, I didn't mean that. I'm sorry."

She stared at the ground and didn't say a word, so he finally walked out the door. He went to his car and slipped into the driver's seat, but didn't start it. Instead, he lay his head back against the headrest of the seat and closed his eyes. That was a mistake, because every time he closed his eyes for the last two weeks, he saw Calla in handcuffs getting escorted out of the airport by two police officers.

Just as he started to reach for the ignition, his phone vibrated. Seeing Mary Anne's number, he answered. "Hey, there, Mary Ann."

"Hello, Samuel." No member of his family ever called him Ian. "I just got off the phone with Calla. I wanted to let you know that the D.A. isn't going to indict her. Now, she and I can go to work clearing her credit and getting her life back."

He clenched his teeth. "Thank you. Thank you for all you've done. That's great news, Mary Ann. Definitely an answer to prayer."

"Amen." She paused before continuing, "This wasn't her fault, you know."

He heaved a heavy sigh. "I know." A flood of emotion had him closing his eyes. "I don't think it's her fault. I just think she should have told me about it before she got arrested."

"It's not easy for a woman to admit to being a victim. We females don't want to appear weak or needy."

He cleared his throat. "I get that, but I think it

becomes a matter of trust at some point. And, I don't think that I can have feelings for someone who doesn't trust me. I have to go. I love you." He hung up the phone before she could reply, and started his car.

Sami scooted closer to Calla in the pew. They looked at the front of the church and not at each other.

"It's finally over," Calla whispered.

"This is good, right?" Sami reached over and took Calla's hand. "We've been praying that it would be over. Why are we sad?" Calla bowed her head. Her body shook with emotion, and Sami squeezed her hand. "I'm sorry that it had to be an arrest, honey, but honestly, you needed a catalyst to make her stop, to make it go away. I think this was honestly the answer to your prayers. You're free now."

She was free. Mary Ann worked on clearing her credit, writing letters and sending documentation. She planned to go back to school in the fall. And yet, instead of relief and joy, she kept hearing Ian's words from last week. "Ian thinks I was with him so he could clear my debt."

Sami let go of her hand and turned to face her fully. "No, he doesn't." She spoke firmly, with conviction in the simple three words.

Calla shrugged with one shoulder. "He said it

himself." Sami didn't speak, so Calla raised her head and looked at her. She had a shocked look on her face. "I could have taken him breaking up with me because I wasn't honest and I was hiding what happened. But to have him say that I made him fall in love with me so that he would write me one big check was horrible. I just—" her breath hitched as she stopped talking. She was so tired of the negative feelings, the tears, the despair.

She surged to her feet and reached behind her to pick her Bible and purse up off the pew. Services had ended more than forty minutes ago. As she left the sanctuary and entered the annex, Sami ran up behind her. "Wait!"

She paused and looked at her best friend. "I just need to work everything out in my head, Sami. I'll be okay. I promise." She hugged her friend. "Thank you."

Sami looped her arm through Calla's as they walked through the church doors. Calla paused and made sure the door locked behind them and slipped a crocheted cap onto her head. Cold January wind blew straight at them, and Calla pulled her wool coat closer around her. Sami gestured at her lone car in the parking lot. "Want a ride?"

Calla considered it, then shook her head. "No. But thanks. I'm going to go get something to eat. I haven't eaten since yesterday."

"Okay. I want to say something." She slipped her hands into the pockets of her fuchsia trench coat and looked up at the sky. "I feel like what you and Ian had was real. I feel like he was really hurt by you not being honest with him and he must have lashed out to say such a fool thing as that. I think you need to consider forgiving him and letting him know that you have." She spoke quickly, saying it all in one breath.

Calla felt a stirring of annoyance at her friend. "I appreciate your honesty. I'll see you tomorrow." She hugged her and turned to walk away without saying anything else.

The cold wind blew into her back, making her rush forward down the sidewalk. A couple blocks away, she pushed into a restaurant and paused for a moment in the warm air while she waited for her glasses to defog. She pulled the hat off her head, and the smells immediately made her realize she'd come to the restaurant where she and Ian had met every Sunday after church throughout their short courtship.

She contemplated leaving, but thinking of the cold wind and the warm interior, she decided to stay. With a smile, she walked toward the hostess stand.

"Hi! Haven't seen you in a couple of weeks," the hostess greeted.

Suddenly missing Ian, she nodded. "I went out of the country for Christmas."

"Well, hon, I hope you had a great time. Your young man is here. Been here about fifteen minutes, I think."

Her stomach fell but, despite the apprehension, she put one foot in front of the other and walked into the restaurant. She spotted Ian at the window table where they always sat. He had a cup of coffee in front of him and stared out of the window.

She slipped into the chair across from him before

speaking. "Hi."

Immediately, he whipped his head around, and his eyes widened when he saw her. "Calla!" His head turned to look out the window before looking at her again. "I was watching for you."

Surprised, she said, "What?"

"I knew you'd walk past here on your way home." He straightened the coffee cup so the handle was perfectly perpendicular to the line of the table. "I, uh, planned to persuade you to come eat with me."

She looked at her watch. "If you've been here long enough for that coffee to be cold, you must have skipped church."

He looked down then back at her. "I was at your church this morning. I wanted to approach you there, but…"

Calla waited then raised an eyebrow. "But?"

He cleared his throat. "But I noticed that you were praying and saw Sami with you. Didn't seem right to intrude."

She felt the broken halves of her heart start to come back together. Ian cared enough about her to not interrupt a time of prayer and meditation. The consideration he'd shown her, that he'd almost always shown her, humbled her. "I see."

"I was about to leave and go to your apartment. When I didn't see you walk by, I thought maybe she'd given you a ride home."

"No. I just stayed for a while." The waitress approached, and Calla ordered food even though she didn't feel hungry. "Do you have something like a beef soup?"

"We have a vegetable beef. It's terrific."

"I'll take a cup. With a roll and some water. Thanks."

The waitress looked at Ian. "You, hon?"

"I'm good with just the coffee. Thanks."

Calla sat back as the waitress left and intentionally kept herself from crossing her arms defensively. "So," she began, toying with the bundle of silverware wrapped in a blue cloth napkin, "you were at my church, and then you were going to come to my apartment? What for, Ian?"

He looked at the coffee in his cup for a long time before looking at her. His eyes looked dull gray-green and red-rimmed with dark circles underneath. Finally, he said, "I sincerely apologize for speaking to you that way. I've spent the last week trying to figure out how to word it so that you would believe me, but all I can say is that I'm sorry."

The waitress brought the water, and Calla asked her, "Can I get some hot tea, too?"

"Sure thing, hon." She looked at Ian. "Want a warm up?"

He didn't speak, but he shook his head and kept his eyes on Calla. When she left, he said, "I don't know why I said what I did, but I didn't mean it, and I don't believe it. I was just really mad at you, I think."

Calla slowly ripped the paper covering off of her straw then tore it into tiny pieces. Using the tip of her finger, she brushed all the pieces into a pile on her placemat. "I knew I should treasure every moment I spent with you because once you found out what had happened to me, you'd not want to be with me anymore."

Ian let out a long sigh. "Calla, you've said that before. But, the truth is, I want to be with you. What hurt me more than anything was that you didn't trust me with the truth."

"Not trust you? It wasn't a lack of trust, Ian. It was a lack of confidence. Confidence in who I am, confidence in who I could be to you. I was embarrassed. No. Not embarrassed." She thought about it. "I was ashamed."

"Ashamed?" He reached forward and took her hand. "Why?"

She stared at their joined hands. "I had spent the last three years paying twenty thousand dollars off of debt that wasn't mine, and prayed daily that she would just die so I didn't have to do it anymore. That day you came and found me crying, she'd just called me to brag about getting a new credit card in my name. I should have recorded the phone call and called the police right then. But I didn't do anything. Except feel sorry for myself and cry."

"Calla—"

She held up a hand to cut off what whatever he planned to say and raised her head to look at him. "I know. Intellectually, I know a lot of things that I'm not able to emotionally face." She took a sip of the water and said without thinking, "Sami said I need to forgive you for saying that to me."

He squeezed her hand and let it go, sitting back so the waitress could bring her soup and tea. She set the heavy soup mug in front of her, made sure she didn't need anything else, then walked away. Calla didn't pick up her spoon. "That wasn't really what I thought. I was just angry and hurt," he admitted, "I'd really appreciate your forgiveness, but I'm not expecting it."

She used the round soup spoon to stir the soup, leaning in to smell the richness of the broth. "I don't think I need to forgive you." At his raised eyebrow, she explained, "I don't think you're the problem. She is. I need to forgive her. I need to forgive her, and I need to learn just what's broken inside of me that allowed me to roll over and let her do what she did since I was a teenager, to just take it and keep taking it the whole time." She dropped the spoon and sat back. "I worked eighty hours a week for two years so I could pay for her thievery, and it was done with such passiveness that the police actually thought I was her partner."

She pushed the soup away, unwilling to risk trying to eat right now. "Why did you use the word broken?" Ian asked.

"What?"

"You said something was broken inside of you. Why did you use that word?"

In her mind, she pictured herself, fractured, colorless, in a gray room without windows. "Isn't that what it is? Whole people don't let someone do that to them without fighting back or at least standing up for themselves, right?"

He sat back, resting his elbows on the arms of the chair and lacing his fingers together. "Hard to say. She catapulted off of your grief. You were an orphan, and she was supposed to have been someone who loved your father."

"Maybe." She considered her father. "But I should have been strong enough to defend him and his memory. Instead, I just—" She cleared her throat. "I need to go."

As she pushed away from the table, he stood with her. "Please stay and talk to me."

She knew if she stepped forward, he would put his arms around her. Instead, she stepped backward, retrieving her coat from the back of her chair. "I don't think I can, right now." She slipped her coat on and pulled her hat out of her pocket. "I appreciate you wanting to defend me and champion me in my circumstances. But, I'm realistically looking at it and don't agree with you. I need to work on me. I need to let God work on me. And I really think I need to do that without the distraction of you trying to work on me." She slipped her purse strap over her head, letting the strap fall across her body. "Goodbye, Ian."

Halfway across the room, she heard him call her name, but she did not stop. "Calla!"

Calla laughed as she chased a soccer ball down the dirt hill. She grabbed it just before it rolled into a thorny brush and held it on her hip as she climbed back up the hill. A group of teenagers waited for her, jabbering to each other in Creole. Calla tossed them the ball and pantomimed to let them know she needed to get a drink of water.

For five months, she'd worked at the little island orphanage in Haiti. She arrived in late February, free from any legal issues and ready to pay Mary Ann back in the most expedient way she could, with her talents and skills. She worked hard cooking for the orphanage, taking local produce and meats and learning from the Haitian cook how to turn them into nutritious meals for the twenty-two children and six adults they fed daily. She'd learned how to operate in a kitchen that had only generator powered electricity, using only products she could obtain regionally. She learned how to prepare foods the kids knew instead of the gourmet fare she'd studied years ago in school. And every day, she'd healed and grown until she could think back to the last four years of her life without feeling persistent pain in her stomach or sharp shame in her heart.

She'd prayed, studied her Bible, prayed, worshiped, prayed, and cooked. The hurricane season had come, and she'd survived a strong category four storm that knocked the school flat and destroyed the generator, leaving them without power for three weeks and a day.

When she had good Internet, she downloaded work projects then transcribed videos and movies and uploaded the finished captions. She made more than enough income to support herself here. Now she faced the end of her time in this beautiful place. She'd received her acceptance back into culinary school. She would start classes in August. It took her a full week to decide that she needed to go back to the United States. Leaving this place behind would hurt. She lessened the pain by promising herself she'd come back again.

She stepped onto the porch and grabbed a bag of water, ripping the corner off with her teeth and drinking all five ounces of the water with three long swallows.

"You're getting better at that game," Hettie Jones remarked from her plastic chair. "One day they might not smear you all over the field."

Calla laughed. "I doubt it, but thanks for the vote of confidence." She looked at her watch. "I should finish getting packed. The truck will be here soon."

Hettie frowned. "I wish you could stay through July. School doesn't start for you until mid-August."

"I need to get settled in Atlanta," Calla said. "It's going to take me some time to reintegrate. I don't want to start school right after coming back. It's going to be hard enough."

"I know. I'm just being selfish. I get to do that sometimes." She stood and hugged her. "I have enjoyed getting to know you better. I hope you come back."

"You would have to try hard to keep me away." She went into the building and walked through the common area to the room she shared with another staff member. She had packed almost everything. Now she added her toothbrush and her laptop. As she zipped the bag closed, she heard the truck pull into the yard.

Taking one last look around the room, at the two cots shrouded with mosquito netting, the small mirror hanging by a rusty nail above a wash basin, and the narrow closet the two women shared, she felt a sense of sorrow at leaving. She had known though, that God brought her here for a short time, not forever. Whatever He had planned for her next waited in Atlanta, not here. Still, she looked forward to returning as soon as possible.

Heaving a sigh, she slung her backpack over one shoulder by a single strap then picked up her duffle bag and walked out of the room, back through the common area, and out onto the porch. She expected to see Emmanuel Danos chatting with his Hettie about their upcoming Christmas wedding as they unloaded supplies he'd picked up at the mainland. She did not expect to see Ian Jones lifting a fifty-pound bag of cornmeal out of the back of the truck.

She resisted the urge to duck back inside the building. Instead, she set her bags down like she originally intended to do and walked over to the truck to help unload.

"Hi, Ian," she greeted as he turned, slinging the heavy bag up onto his shoulder.

He stopped moving and stared at her, from braided hair to her leather sandals. "Sounds like I almost missed you," he said by way of greeting, banishing any thought that he didn't know about her presence here for the last several months.

"A day later and you would have." She felt nerves, familiar nerves, like the kind that had assaulted her the first time she cooked dinner for him.

They unloaded the truck in silence with Hettie and Emmanuel. A million things she wanted to say to him ran through her mind, but she couldn't find the right opening, so she just lifted, carried, and stacked bags and boxes in the storeroom. Once they had emptied the truck, Ian collected her bags from the porch and put her tote bag into the bed and her backpack into the cab of the truck. Calla hugged Hettie, tight. "I can't wait until next time," she said.

"Looking forward to it. Next time I'm in Atlanta, I hope to be able to experience what you do with your own ingredients in a modern kitchen. You've been an amazing help here, and we will miss you like you can't even know."

She turned toward Ian and extended her hand. "I'd love to stay and spend time with you, but I can't."

He smiled a half smile and shook her hand perfunctorily. "I know." He turned to Emmanuel and said something in Creole. The men shook hands warmly, and Emmanuel tossed Ian the keys. Emmanuel waved at Calla and put his arm over Hettie's shoulders, leading her into the building.

Calla frowned as Ian turned to her. "Ready?"

"For?"

"To leave." He walked to the truck and climbed into the driver's seat. Calla began to understand that he would drive her to the ferry. It took her several minutes to get to the truck, though, because as she walked forward, the children surrounded her. She took the time to speak to each one, hug everyone, and make a personal connection with every child. By the time she disengaged from them, she had tears pouring down her face. How could she leave?

Knowing she must, she slipped into the passenger's seat. Ian started the truck, and she shifted her backpack to rest behind the seat as she snapped her seatbelt into place. "This is harder than I thought."

"Every time." He slowly drove down the dirt lane, carefully avoiding potholes. "I spent a year here in between high school and college. I'm still not sure how I managed to leave willingly."

The truck bounced over a rut, so he slowed down even more. "You're not supposed to be here," she finally said. "It's July."

He spared her a quick but serious glance. "I wanted to see you. I didn't want to wait anymore. I had no idea you'd leave so soon."

He wanted to see her? Her heart started pounding, and she licked dry lips. "I…" She looked out the window and watched the island jungle crawl slowly by as Ian navigated over the lava rock path.

"You wish I'd never come." The truck jostled roughly, and he hit the brakes, stopping it entirely. He turned his body toward her. "If you didn't want to have anything at all to do with me, you would have found another place to work, another orphanage, another mission, another country even. The fact is, you needed the connection with my family."

"Leaving engineering behind to become a shrink?" She crossed her arms over her chest. Not because she wanted to shield herself from him, but because she knew he spoke the truth and it made her feel defensive. "I'm here because I spent the last five months paying Mary Ann back for her brilliant legal services. That was our deal. She represented me and will continue to fight collection agencies and credit reporting agencies, and I cook for Hettie and Emmanuel. So what?"

"So what is I'm here. That's what," He lay his arm over the steering wheel and his other arm over the back of the seat, boxing her in. She wanted to reach forward and touch him, but kept her arms tight around her chest. "And I've missed you. This month is the eight-month anniversary of the day you sent me flowers—the day I began the journey of falling in love with you." Her breath hitched, and she opened her mouth to speak, but no words came out. He'd mentioned love twice now. "Don't you tell me that wasn't God's providence. You and I both know otherwise."

She unbuckled the seatbelt and leaned back against the door, pulling her legs up. Her forehead fell forward and rested on her knees. "I know," she whispered. "I needed to come here. I needed to get close to God and work my way through the years since my father died. I had to come to a place of forgiveness for Becky, or whatever her real name is, and I had to mean it. I didn't want it to be a hollow promise because God would know the difference."

Several seconds went by in silence. She raised her head and found him staring at her, his hazel eyes serious and searching. Finally, he said, "And me?"

"Ian, I don't know about you, or us. I wanted to talk to you when I got home, but I didn't even think you'd want to see me. I need to get home and figure things out."

He started the truck again and slowly inched forward. She straightened in the seat and latched her seatbelt. After a few seconds, he said, "I appreciate that, but I feel like that's what you've been doing, here. I took off work and made a two-day trip to see you. I've given you space, and I've given you time. I honestly don't know how much more space and time I'm willing to give you."

She sat in silence for several minutes and finally said, "I respect that. Thanks for your honesty."

They didn't speak again until they finished the descent down the mountain and pulled onto the coastal road. Too soon, he pulled into the parking lot for the ferry.

"Pastor Jeremy Banks will meet you at the ferry," he said, opening the driver's door. She slipped out of the truck and reached back into the cab to get her backpack. "He's made arrangements for you to stay at the mission in Port-au-Prince overnight, and he'll give you a ride to the airport tomorrow."

He handed her the tote bag. She set it on the ground and stepped closer to him, putting her arms around him. She could feel his hesitation before he hugged her back. "I miss you," she said quietly. "Thank you for the ride."

"Bye, Calla." She picked up her tote and walked to the ferry, unwilling to look behind her.

CHAPTER 9

Calla heard her alarm going off, but tried to bury under the covers and ignore it. No luck. Ignoring it didn't make it stop.

As she sat up, she grabbed her phone and turned the alarm off. 5:32. Had she seriously managed to ignore it for two whole minutes?

It didn't take long to throw on a pair of jeans and a long-sleeved T-shirt. She went into the bathroom and washed her face, leaning close to the mirror to stare into her own eyes as she dried her skin. She'd stayed up late studying and her red-rimmed eyes showed it. This fatigue, though, compared to the fatigue she'd felt a year ago, felt good, productive, like she could look forward to a good end after all of her hard work.

She braided her hair into a tight plait, then walked back through her bedroom, scooping her glasses off of the dresser and slipping them on her face. In the living room, she went to her desk and pulled the stack of papers off her printer, then punched holes in them to put them in her binder. Today, she had an exam, and she knew that the chef would check the binders to make sure that they contained all of the recipes, properly written, neatly typed with clear instructions.

While she sat on the couch to tie her shoes, she mentally went through the lessons the day before and the recipes she'd typed up. They'd served a venison medallion with three different purees: chestnut, carrot, and celery root. She'd fallen in love with the chestnut puree, and so very much wanted to take the time to perfect it in her home kitchen. Maybe she could do something at Thanksgiving with it.

Thoughts of Thanksgiving immediately brought Ian to mind. She thought about how relaxed and happy he'd been, sitting at Annabelle's table while she got to know his family. Her stomach fluttered with nerves at the thought of him. She'd wanted to call him for weeks now. Why did she keep hesitating? Fear of rejection?

She sat back against the cushions and closed her

eyes, leaning her head back until it rested on the back of the couch. She had regretted leaving Ian in Haiti the moment she stepped onto the deck of the ferry. It had taken all of her will to not turn around and go back to the island and beg his forgiveness for doubting herself for even a moment. Yet, despite regrets, she constantly felt like she truly had needed to leave. She needed to discover the true Calla Vaughn.

She'd worn the hats of an adored child of a single parent, a despised step-daughter, an exhausted culinary student working her way through her first year as an independent adult, a grieving orphan, and a victim of a con artist who currently faced charges in three states. She'd never had an opportunity to live, on her own, without suffocating under grief or fear. It felt like God-given wisdom to allow herself to take time alone, back in familiar surroundings, older and much wiser.

It didn't take long for her to realize that the Calla she knew still existed—only this Calla had much more confidence and faith. She should have called Ian right away, but had just not. Why?

Had God kept her from reaching out? How many times had she walked past his church on a Sunday morning, wanting to go in and slide into the chair next to him? How often had she considered just ringing his doorbell? Despite this constant wanting to contact him, she had always pulled back.

This morning, though, more than ever, she felt a pull to call him. "God," she said softly, "this is the part where I need to hear Your voice. I need to know what to do next."

Her phone vibrated and she saw the notice for her daily Bible thought that came at 5:45 every day. Today's verse said:

And no one puts new wine into old wineskins; or else the new wine will burst the wineskins and be spilled, and the wineskins will be ruined. But new wine must be put into new wineskins, and both are preserved.

Luke 5:37-38

Pursing her lips, she considered the words. An answer to prayer, or was she reading into it?

As she gathered her knife bag and put her binder and clean uniform into her backpack, she thought about the verse. What did it mean? What could it mean to her in this present circumstance?

She lived just a few blocks from the school, so she walked in the predawn darkness along the quiet street, meditating about Ian. The few weeks they spent as a couple, they received constant affirmation from people around them—Christians and non-Christians alike. Despite age differences, background differences, and other things, they had made a good couple, a strong couple, a mission-minded couple with a love for people and God. How could anyone consider that a bad thing?

But she'd waited so long. Should she have stayed in Haiti with him, or begged him to come back with her?

No. No time for regrets. Right now, she faced a new start. She had long considered this school year the beginning of the beginning.

"In the beginning, Calla shed her insecurities and fear and stepped boldly forward to accomplish her goals and dreams." She'd said that out loud as she walked out of the Atlanta airport in late July, fresh from her time in Haiti. And, she'd meant it. She said it again this morning to remind herself of her forward motion.

No insecurities or fears.

She entered the side door of the school and nodded to fellow culinary students. In the locker room, she put on her uniform and wrapped a hot-pink bandana around her head. She spent the next hour and a half prepping the chef's *mis en place* for the coming lesson, peeling head after head of garlic, chopping shallots, and gathering supplies and equipment from the commissary. The entire time she worked, she kept saying that Bible verse over and over again in her head. *But new wine must be put into new wineskins, and both are preserved.*

Hours later, after serving the head of the school a medallion of lamb served with roasted Brussels sprouts and a potato dish called *pommes roesti*, she joined the other students outside at the picnic tables. Despite the hot sun, the wind picked up and blew cool air. Calla quickly moved her plate out of the shade and into full sun, taking another small bite and analyzing the sauce she'd put on the lamb. An oak leaf floated past her plate, reminding her again of Ian, of autumn, of the time they'd spent through Christmas.

She'd kept in touch with Mary Ann, hoping that the attorney would pass along her new address and her new phone number. She knew he knew she was at school right there in Atlanta. However, she'd heard nothing from him. She'd hoped that he might reach out to her just one more time. even though the two prior times he had, she'd turned him away. While she hadn't flat out rejected him, she had asked him to wait until she was ready. He'd told her very point blank that he didn't know how long he could wait. Now she worried too much time had gone by, and what stretched between them now was a chasm that she didn't know if she had the strength or the tools to cross.

A chasm that he may not want her to cross.

She had to consider that he might have closed his mind and heart to her forever. She also had to consider that he might have found someone else by now. If it was true, then she only had herself to blame. Accepting that didn't make the thought any easier to bear, didn't make the ache in her heart at the thought lessen in any way. But, the idea of him fully rejecting her hurt worse with a pain that seared through her heart and deep into her soul.

That was what kept her from reaching out. However, the longer she gave into that hesitation, that insecurity, the more likely an outcome that ended in Ian turning her away. Every minute she held herself back was a minute lost to them together. She could see that and hated the reluctance born of an insecure persona she purposefully shed months ago. Stepping forward boldly—she intentionally used those words to strengthen her resolve in everything in life. So why hesitate now?

She mulled that question over as she pushed her plate away. She only hesitated out of fear. She would not stand for that. Time to span that chasm.

Knowing full well that she must contact him, she thought about how to go about doing just that. If she called, would he answer the phone? If she rang his doorbell, would he open the door to her? She thought about the first time he came to her home for dinner, about the administrative mistake at a flower shop that brought them together—that they both believed that God used to bring them together. What would he do if a bouquet of flowers walked through his doorway with a note on them asking him to dinner?

She gasped out loud, then looked around to see if anyone noticed. Should she? What if—

What if she sent him flowers and he ignored her? What if he didn't, though? What if he felt a nostalgic pull to the idea of her stepping boldly out in faith and restarting their relationship, or even the possibility of restarting their relationship?

Doing something so fantastically crazy might be exactly what he needed her to do. It would give him time alone to process the idea of her invitation, without the pressure of her standing in front of him or waiting for a word form him on the other end of the telephone. He could think about it, pray about it, and determine if he had the desire in his heart to accept the hand she reached out to him letting him know that she wanted to be with him, that she wanted a reset.

He could choose to toss the flowers into the trash and

ignore the invite, but he could also choose to accept at the invitation and show up with their future in his hands.

Giving in to the impulse, she pulled her phone out of her pocket and looked up the number for Crossroads Florists. Calling the toll-free number, she turned so that her back was to her fellow students.

"Out of the Blue Bouquet," a woman with a very happy and pleasant voice said, "this is Brooke. How may I help you?"

Calla's stomach nervously twisted. "Hi. Didn't I call Crossroads?"

"Yes, ma'am. You sure did. How can I help you?"

Calla cleared her throat, "I, uh, sent flowers a year ago today. Could, um, could you maybe look them up and re-send the same bouquet?"

She could hear the clicking of keys on the keyboard as Brooke answered her. "Absolutely. Let's see if we can find you. What phone number would those have been ordered under?"

Ian tossed the pencil down and closed his eyes, rolling his head on his neck. He couldn't concentrate, and he grew steadily impatient with it all. Before Calla, he could always shut out the world and just work. Not anymore. For months now, he had to battle thoughts of dark brown eyes.

Last week, the long Georgia summer had finally released the reins of sunshine and the air reluctantly started cooling down. With a cold wind, the leaves began falling from trees. Immediately, he thought of Calla Vaughn and her mustard-colored scarf and earth brown boots.

He wondered if she'd settled back into the student routine at the culinary school. He wondered what her days looked like and what her heart felt like and whether she had worked her way through all the stuff going on in her brain that kept her from just allowing something good to happen in her life. He felt impatient, and a little bit angry, but mostly just done with waiting.

No one would ever know how often he drove past the school, hoping for a chance meeting. He'd watched with rapt attention at a bid that Dixon Brothers put in to build a new building for the college. When they didn't get it, he felt personally affected. Now, he stared down the unsatisfying time of the coming week before Thanksgiving and realized that he had a season full of memories to experience and get past so he could hopefully start to get over her.

He heard the knock on his door and looked at his watch. Penny wasn't due back from lunch for another fifteen minutes. "Come in," he called, not moving from his perch at his drafting table.

When a large bouquet of flowers in the colors of fall came through his door, his stomach fell, and he immediately got up to intercept them.

"Let me," he said, relieving them from the teenager's

arms.

"Delivery for Ian Jones," the boy said.

"Thanks," Ian replied, quickly setting the flowers on his desk and digging through the fall colored blooms to find the card.

"Happy Thanksgiving," the boy said as he ducked out of the office.

Ian retrieved the note from the plastic prongs, his heart racing.

DINNER AT 6:30 TONIGHT. MY PLACE. WON'T TAKE NO. CALLA

He read her new address, recognizing a street close to the school. He hadn't bothered to look up her new address upon his return from Haiti. Mary Ann had informed him that Calla had moved but Ian hadn't asked to where and she hadn't volunteered the information. He suspected Mary Ann just wanted him to know she had Calla's new address in the event Ian ever wanted to look her up again. Fine and good, but in the nearly four months since Calla had returned to Atlanta, Ian had not wanted to see her, and she had not made any effort to reach out to him.

Until today.

Almost like one of those sappy climactic scenes in a romantic movie where the guy flashes back to the pivotal moments he and the heroine have shared, a private movie played out in his memory. He remembered the first time he really took notice of her that day they shared the elevator after her car died. He remembered the way she moved as she hummed and danced in the filing room. He remembered her cheeks blushing the first time they held hands which happened to also be the first time they prayed together, asking God to bless their first shared meal. He remembered the taste of that first meal and he could not erase the image of her chocolate eyes or her uncensored smile.

He remembered how she loved on every single child at the orphanage. He watched as her heart nearly broke leaving Haiti behind when returning from that first mission trip. He imagined just how she would pour love and nurturing care into her own children one day.

He remembered the way she smelled when they hugged. He remembered the first time he had kissed her, the feel of her soft lips beneath his, and the scent of homemade apple pie when the kiss ended.

He also remembered her shocked pale face as she was introduced to handcuffs at the Atlanta airport. In that moment more than any other, he felt a giant fracture crack through any future plans that may have involved her. Up until that moment, his plans involved flirting with her and courting her in a way far superior to any other men who may have come into her life before. He never had any idea he might end up forking over bail money or writing out a sworn statement for the Superior Court. He never could have imagined courting Calla might involve actual courts of law.

He remembered her angry, defensive words as she tried to justify her deception. Shamefully, he also remembered his own angry words, and wished for the hundredth time he had never spoken them into the world. He remembered asking for her forgiveness, trying to mend fences. He had hoped she would see the sincerity in his heart and lean on him and his strength. He had hoped they could continue to build on their relationship and rebuild the trust. Instead, she had left him cooling his heels. She fled to Haiti for five months, which may as well have been a lifetime on the moon.

He had reached out to her so many times, only to get silence or some blow off response. He had decided that when he went to Haiti weeks early so they could have some one-on-one time to see what, if anything, could happen next between them, that would be the end of it. One way or another, he would know if they had a future before he came back home. If anything, the way Calla left things between them the last time he saw her should have decided it once and for all.

So, what was the deal with this invitation? The flowers? The won't take no for an answer when all she had given him for nearly a year now was no kind of answer at all? Did she think he was some kind of safety net? Come over and play boyfriend but only when it was convenient?

Or did he dare hope she might have really changed? Had she come to some kind of realization after all this time? At this point, with so much water under the bridge, could they have a future? Was this her idea of a let's settle this thing once-and-for-all like Haiti had been for him?

If so, did she deserve one more chance? Or not. Won't take no? What if he just went home and forgot all about Calla Vaughn? What then? Would his life finally resume without visions of chocolate brown eyes constantly distracting him?

As he tossed the card on the desk, his door opened again, and Al came striding in. "You up for some lunch?" He stopped when he saw the flowers on the desk. "I'm feeling a bit of a déjà vu."

"Yeah. Me, too." Ian ran a finger over the petal of a mum. "The only real question is, do I go or not?"

"I think you know the answer to that, brother." Al slapped him on the back of his shoulders. "I think all of us in your life right now pray that you go and that things get worked out one way or the other."

"What does that mean?"

"That means our dinner plans are officially canceled, and I'll see you tomorrow."

Ian took a deep breath. "I don't think so, man."

Al crossed his arms. "What does that mean?"

Ian shrugged. "I don't think I'm willing to go, to open back up."

Al sat on the stool at Ian's drafting table. "Let me tell you something, brother. I know her lack of trust hurt you. I get that from here to tomorrow. But, I also respect the fact that she very openly told you about her need to find out who she really is before she could be with you. She didn't ask for five years, and she didn't even wait six months. You ask me? I think this is a good thing."

Knowing that Al had suffered a broken heart made him narrow his eyes. "You say that knowing how it feels..." his voice trailed off, unable or unwilling to delve into the intricacies of Al's tumultuous relationship with his sister.

"How it feels to have my heart cut out of my chest?" Al barked a short, humorless laugh. "Yeah, bro. I am. You and Calla, man, you two fit. I think you just need to let last year go and start fresh, you know. Begin again, with all the hurt and pain and angst that has driven you into the ground since the New Year just gone, not to return."

Ian unconsciously mimicked Al by crossing his arms. "A fresh start, huh?"

Al walked across the office and pulled the chair out from Ian's drafting table. He rotated it around and straddled it, resting his arms across the back of the chair. "Sometimes you have to forgive and forget. Start over. Think about this, man. What if...?"

Ian waited but Al didn't finish the sentence. After a few seconds he looked up to meet his friend's gaze. The look in Al's eye made it clear that he was about to ask something he felt was important. Al nodded. "What if God made her for you and made you for her? You still up for standing her up then?"

Ian's gaze fell and he studied the toes of his shoes. "I thought that before, you know. That first time we went to Haiti? How she was with the kids? I thought to myself, this is the one for me. I praised God that he could make someone so beautiful and kind and all I had to do was make her mine." He smiled at the memory. "Then we came back from Haiti and everything changed."

"Well," Al chuckled. "Every relationship has its ups and downs."

"Funny." Ian didn't laugh.

"Oh, so you think you're some prize? Brother, let me just drop a few truth bombs on you. You have momma and daddy issues a mile high from losing your folks so young. You're moody. You can get way too focused on things. And you're just a little bit judgmental of the blue-collar types in that oh-so-special old money kind of way. Did you know that?"

"That's raw, man."

"Hey, I love you. But you have to know you have your own baggage, too. This girl was terrorized by her stepmother. She didn't have a rich grandmother to take her in." Al held up a halting hand when he saw Ian tense up, realizing he was dancing on a line he didn't want to cross. "The point is that she's reaching out to you, now. Something made her do that. Maybe she just feels sorry for you, I don't know. Or maybe God has been working on her, too. A lot of people have been praying for her."

Ian thought about that. Could he possibly forgive and forget like nothing had happened? Did he want to? "That's what I need to do."

"What? Go to dinner?"

Ian grinned a toothless grin. "Maybe. But right now, I need to pray. I need to ask God to speak to my heart." He looked up and met Al's eyes. "Pray with me?"

"Thought you'd never ask."

"Are you sure about this?" Sami asked. She stood in the middle of Calla's apartment wearing a maroon jumper miniskirt over a blouse covered in gold and maroon cartoon turkeys. She had a beanie cap perched on the back of her head and ankle-high black boots. "He's not the same person he was a year ago."

"Neither am I." Calla spread the tablecloth over her little round table and brushed her hand across the top, smoothing out a wrinkle here and a fold there. She'd hoped that the tablecloth she'd used on the card table almost precisely a year ago would fit on her table. It almost did, well enough to use it.

"No. You've really gained some confidence I've never seen before. I like it."

They set out chargers, plates, and napkins secured with sunflower rings. When the table looked perfect, Sami picked up the box she'd brought over. "I'm just going to set this in your room. Load everything back up, and I'll pick it up after church Sunday."

Calla met her at the bedroom door. "I really appreciate your help. I wish I had a way to repay you for all the times you've been right there, helping me."

Sami laughed and hugged Calla. "You say that like you've never cooked for me in your life. Girl, you've got it backward." She pulled away and looked at Calla with serious eyes. "I'm worried tonight won't go well."

Calla's stomach turned and twisted. She walked into the kitchen and Sami followed. Here, she had confidence. Here, she could excel and not fail. Outside of the kitchen, she'd made a shamble of her life. In here, though...

She pulled the towel off of the loaf of bread and pressed her finger into it, checking to see if it had risen long enough. The indentation remained, so she set the oven to heat up. As she worked, she considered her words.

"I know that I hurt Ian. But I also know that I needed this time. It's up to him to accept that." She looked at her friend. "Or not. But I have to give him a chance to definitively end it."

"And if he doesn't show?"

"That would be rather definitive, would it not?" The idea hurt her heart, but in all fairness, she half expected that to happen. "I prayed for an end to my problems. God provided it. Now I'm praying for God's guidance here, and he gave me this verse, *But new wine must be put into new wineskins, and both are preserved.* I can only rest in the hope that God is telling me that Ian and I should start fresh, start over, not go back." She smiled. "Whatever happens, reaching out was the right thing to do."

"Seeing how God worked out the thing with your stepmother makes me believe that if you asked for a word from Him, He'd totally give it to you. Some people would just take any sign that pointed in the direction they wanted to go as the word from God. You? I think you're something special." Sami picked her purse up off of the kitchen counter. "I can't wait to see you at church Sunday. Do me a favor and shoot me a text tonight before bed. Give me a little glimpse of what happened?"

"Deal."

After walking Sami to the door, she slipped the bread into the oven then went into her bedroom and opened the closet door. Since she wore a uniform to school, she had so few items to wear. She settled on a cotton, long-sleeved dress the color of sage that fell to just above the knee, camel-colored knee-high boots, and a lilac and sage scarf. Before she could put her makeup on, the timer for the bread went off. She looked at her watch. 6:25. Rushing through the apartment, she pulled the bread out of the oven and set it on the stove to cool, then went to her bathroom to put on makeup.

Just as she applied the coat of pink lipgloss, the doorbell rang promptly at 6:30. Calla looked around the apartment one last time, seeing everything still in order. Would he notice how much everything resembled their dinner a year ago, down to the cushions on the couch?

She put a hand on her fluttering stomach, breathed out through her nose, then opened the door. He wore a pair of khaki pants and a dark green button-down shirt that made his eyes shine with a green light. A smile broke across her face at the sight of him, but his expression remained stoic in response.

"Hi there," she said, opening the door so that he could come in. "I wondered if you'd come."

"That right? Well, I reckon I did too." He kept his

hands in his pockets as he entered the apartment. She watched him look around, with his eyes resting several spare moments on the table decorated with sunflowers. She wondered if he could recognize the smell of chicken Florentine cooking in the oven. "Still not sure I wanted to, but I'm here."

She gestured at the couch and said, "We have about ten minutes before dinner's ready."

"I can come back," Ian turned back toward the door.

"I'd like to talk if that's okay," Calla said quickly.

A muscle ticked in his jaw, and he stiffly stalked across the room and sat at the end of the couch. She sat at the other end, turning toward him. She had worked out what she wanted to say all day, but she didn't know how to begin. Did she just start by apologizing, maybe begging, maybe pleading? Would throwing herself at his feet fix the ache in his heart that had to mirror the pain in her soul?

Not knowing where to start, she began with, "I spent the few weeks we were together knowing that it would eventually end. I wouldn't burden you with my debt, and I didn't see a way out of it. I feel like my desperate prayer to God about it is what led to my arrest. I say that in hindsight because, in the midst of it, I was overcome with despair. But the arrest was the catalyst to free me from it all, which was exactly my prayer."

He kept his eyes forward, staring at a spot on the wall, not even looking at her, so she kept speaking. "Keeping that to myself the entire time wasn't fair to you. I've spent the last several months remembering every word, every touch, every expression. And, again, separated from it, in hindsight, I can believe that you would have seen me through anything. Not giving you that opportunity to lead me through it wasn't fair to you, and I would like to ask you for your forgiveness."

At her words, his head whipped around, and he stared at her in stony silence for a long time, his lips thin, his eyes hard. She held her breath, desperately wishing he would relax and smile and open his arms. Finally, he said, "I don't know."

"That's fair." She gestured at the table. "I would very much like a reset. I want you to be able to get to know me without a sixty-thousand-dollar secret affecting my every thought and word. I want you to let the real Calla Vaughn into your life, and maybe you'll fall in love with the real me the same way I fell in love with the real you." She paused, and her breath hitched. She clasped her hands tightly together.

He closed his eyes as if looking at her fatigued him. She held her breath, worried that he'd just flat out reject her and then where would she be? Lost. Without direction. Hopeless.

When he opened his eyes again, his expression had softened. He slowly lifted his arm and held out his hand, palm up. Without hesitation, she placed her hand in his and let him pull her close. She breathed in the familiar smell of him as his arms came around her. "I think I would like that very much," he said, his voice vibrating against her ear. She lifted her face to look at him and caught a glimpse of a promise of a beautiful future in his eyes as his lips covered hers.

THE END

The Dixon Brothers Series:

Courting Calla: Dixon Brothers book 1

Ian knows God has chosen Calla as the woman for him, but Calla is hiding something big. Can Calla trust Ian with her secret, or will she let it destroy any possible hope for a future they may have?

Valerie's Verdict: Dixon Brothers book 2

Since boyhood days, Brad has always carried a flame for Valerie. Her engagement to another man shattered his dreams. When she comes home, battered and bruised, recovering from a nearly fatal relationship, he prays God will use him to help her heal.

Alexandra's Appeal: Dixon Brothers book 3

Jon falls very quickly in love with Alex's zest for life and her perspective of the the world around her. He steps off of his path to be with her. When forces move against them and rip them apart, he wants to believe God will bring them back together, but it might take a miracle.

Daisy's Decision: Dixon Brothers book 4

Daisy has had a crush on Ken since high school, so going on just one date with him can't possibly hurt, can it? Even if she's just been painfully dumped by the man she planned to spend the rest of her life with, and whose unborn baby she carries? Just one date?

Excerpt from Book 2

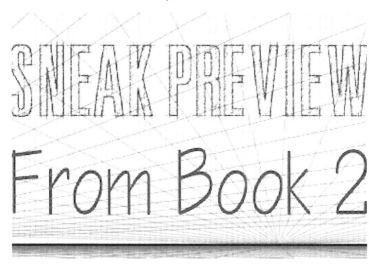

Valerie's Virdict

Please enjoy this sneak peek excerpt from *Valerie's Verdict*, book 2 in the Dixon Brothers Series.

Using her **ID badge, Valerie** keyed into the Dixon Contracting building and walked across the nearly empty lobby. The large Roman numeral clock that hung on the wall behind the security desk told her that she'd made it in just before six-thirty. Most of her floor didn't get in until eight, so she'd have time to get a lot of work done before the busyness of the day interrupted. Once inside the elevator, the door started to close when a hand stopped it. A second later, Brad Dixon stepped into the car.

"Good morning, Valerie," he said, smiling with perfectly straight teeth. "I was hoping to catch you first thing."

She felt an eyebrow raise and the tension she'd felt in her neck shot down her entire spine. "Oh?"

"Yup. Drop by my office before heading to yours."

That was Brad. Message delivered. Message received. She remembered playing with him as a child. He was always very serious, taking charge of the playtime with his brothers, organizing toys just so, sticking to the rules no matter the game, always acting like the oldest, even though as triplets, they were all the same age. She imagined that his father had no hesitation in naming him the head of the company because maturity had only honed those natural inclinations into a man designed for that role.

"Sure," she answered, smiling a bit as she remembered a swimming pool warmed by the hot Georgia sun. She'd worn a pink bathing suit with purple hearts on it, and remembered her childhood amazement at how dark the normally light skinned triplets got by the end of the summer. Ken, or maybe Jon, had joked that they'd be as dark as her before long. She remembered thinking they were kind of crazy boys.

"This way," he said, as the elevator stopped on the tenth floor. She found herself back where she'd been the night before, walking past the same receptionist area, through the same deserted hallway. They turned a corner, and she saw Philip's name on the brass sign beside the door. Down another hallway, they stopped at the corner office, and Brad pulled a key out of his pocket. "Just in here," he said, though it was a redundant statement since the brass plaque next to this door read, "BRADFORD DIXON."

Just inside that door, they walked into an office that housed a young woman with black hair wearing a shiny blue blouse and a necklace of large, bright yellow flowers. Three empty chairs separated by small square tables sat, obviously a waiting area of some sort. Valerie was surprised to see someone here so early.

"Good morning, Sami," he greeted as the door softly shut behind them. "Coffee, please."

"Good morning, Brad" she greeted with a smile, putting down the files she'd had in her hand when the door opened. "I'll be right there with it. Just finished brewing."

He led Valerie through the door behind Sami's desk, and she entered his office. A small conference table that could accomodate eight people sat on one side of the entrance, and a little seating area with a small couch and a short coffee table sat in another. Across the room, a massive desk sat in front of the corner windows that looked out at Atlanta's skyline. Her practiced eyes skimmed over the leather furniture, bold colors, and tasteful paintings, silently approving of the design job.

"Please, sit down," he said, gesturing at the couch. Before she could decline, Sami returned carrying a tray coffee, cups, sugar, creamer, and a small dish of shortbread cookies. She set the tray on the coffee table and left the room without a word.

Brad poured coffee into one of the cups and handed it to her. Instinctively, she took it. "Brad…" she began, but she stuttered and stopped.

He waited, then finally prompted her with, "Yes?"

She cleared her throat. "I just want to apologize for last night."

He raised an eyebrow. "Apologize?"

That tripped her up. "Yes. Apologize."

"For what?"

Her eyebrows drew together in a frown. "Well, uh, I imagine for getting in that gentleman's way."

"That right?" With pursed lips, he stared at her for a few seconds before he asked, "Did you often have to apologize for getting in Tyrone's way?"

Shame warred with anger inside her chest. Gripping the coffee cup in her hands tightly, she lifted her chin. "I will not discuss it."

His gray eyes stared at her for several seconds, a serious, contemplative look. Finally, he, too, set his cup down. "Dixon Contracting takes care of its employees. We provide housing when needed, as I know you know.

We provide tuition assistance, certification expenses, good benefits. All of that is for employees."

"I'm not a new employee, Brad. I've worked for you for years."

"Yes, you have." He leaned forward and laced his fingers, propping his elbows on his knees. "Thing is, that's how we take care of our employees. You, however, we regard as family. You stayed in our home as many nights as your own until you moved off to Savannah. My mother did a good portion of raising you, and your uncle Buddy's my father's best friend. As such, if there's ever anything you need, no matter what, no matter the hour, we're here for you. And for Buddy. I just want to make sure you remember that."

She let that soak in while she studied the sincere look on his face. "It's funny. In the last few days, I've had so many memories return to me. Things I shouldn't have forgotten about. Swimming with you guys, exploring in the woods behind your house, eating in that gigantic kitchen with the cook slipping us extra scoops of ice cream when your mama wasn't looking. I haven't thought of it for years. I don't know if homesickness made me shut it all out or what, but it's good to be here. It's good to be home." She slowly stood, being careful of her hip with that movement. "Thank you for the coffee and for reaching out. I appreciate it."

Brad stood, too, and despite the way he towered over her by a good foot, she didn't feel the need to shrink away from him. He pulled a business card out of his pocket and held it out to her. "If you need anything, please call me."

Hesitating only a second, she took the card from him and smiled. "Do your parents still live in the castle?"

Phillip often told the story of standing on the banks of the Chattahoochee River near the little Georgia town where they grew up, promising Rosaline that if she would run away with him to Atlanta, he would build her a castle and she would be his queen. Brad and his family moved into the newly constructed castle when he and his brothers were five. She had so much fun with Brad and his triplet brothers, growing up there, exploring the grounds, finding the hidden passages that the design team had worked in. He grinned. "Not only do they still live there, they're ready to fill it with grandchildren if my brothers and I would just cooperate."

Familiarity with him and his family filled her. She no longer felt uncomfortable, out of place. She smiled. "I'd love to see it again. I should give your mama a call."

"You should come over tonight. We'll have dinner. Mama would be thrilled."

Remembering the big dining room with the portrait of Phillip and Rosaline hanging on the wall behind the head of the table, she smiled. "I think I'd like that very much."

"Great. I'll find out the best time and let you know."

He walked her to the door and opened it. Just as she started to walk past him, he said very quietly, "Don't ever apologize for what someone else did to you again, Valerie."

Startled, she looked up at him, their bodies close, and could see the anger simmering in the edges of his eyes. Her mouth dry, she simply nodded and walked into Sami's office.

READERS GUIDE
Questions

S uggested **discussion group questions** for *Courting Calla* by Hallee Bridgeman.

When asking ourselves how important the truth is to our Creator, we can look to the reason Jesus said he was born. In the book of John 18:37, Jesus explains that *for this reason He was born and for this reason He came into the world.* The reason? To testify to the truth.

In bringing those He ministered to into an understanding of the truth, Our Lord used fiction in the form of parables to illustrate very real truths. In the same way, we can minister to one another by the use of fictional characters and situations to help us to reach logical, valid, cogent, and very sound conclusions about our real lives here on earth.

While the characters and situations in The Dixon Brothers Series are fictional, I pray that these extended parables can help readers come to a better understanding of truth. Please prayerfully consider the questions that follow, consult scripture, and pray upon your conclusions. May the Lord of the universe richly bless you.

Calla and Ian both believe that God orchestrated the mix-up in the flower delivery that brought them together.

1) Do you think that God actually plays such an active part in our lives so as to arrange people to meet in such a way?

2) Can you think of a time when that happened to you—a time when you're certain God had a hand in it?

Calla prayed for God to release her from the debt in which her stepmother had maliciously placed her. The end result was that Calla was arrested on the suspicion of passing $10,000 worth of bad checks. It caused a spiral that, despite the terrible moments, ended up freeing her from the debt—which was an answer to prayer.

> 3) Romans 8:28 says, *For God works together for good all things for those who love Him and are called according to His purpose.* Do you think that this is an example of God working together for good all things as they pertained to Calla?

> 4) Or, do you think that God answered Calla's prayer by orchestrating her arrest?

Ian believes that if Calla had been honest with him at any time during the brief beginning of their relationship, he would have supported her.

> 5) Given an idea of Ian's personality, do you think he would have supported her, or was he

speaking in hindsight?

6) Do you think Ian's faith was strong enough to believe that if God had indeed brought them together, he *should* have supported her and therefore would have?

Calla asked Ian to give her time to get to know the "real" Calla before she would be free to pursue a relationship with him.

7) What do you think her real motivation was?

8) Do you think this was fair to Ian considering he'd come so far to show her how much he cared?

9) Do you think that Calla's decision showed a lack of her own faith in trusting God's answers to her prayers?

Calla did not file charges against her stepmother and

instead subjected herself to tens of thousands of dollars of debt that SHE chose to pay off.

10) What do you think you would do in the event that a family member stole your identity?

11) Do you think that filing charges would have been the right thing to do right away, or should Calla have given her stepmother a chance to stop what she was doing and pay her back?

12) Do you consider the theft of the identity of a family member a crime, or an inconvenience? Would you consider the relationship with the family member more important than justice?

NOTES: _____

_____

_____

_____

_____

_____

_____

READERS GUIDE

Recipes

Suggested **luncheon menu to enjoy** when hosting a group discussion for *Courting Calla*.

Those who followed my Hallee the Homemaker website know that one thing I am passionate about in life is selecting, cooking, and savoring good whole real food. A special luncheon just goes hand in hand with hospitality and ministry.

For those planning a discussion group about this book, I offer some humble suggestions to help your special luncheon conversation come off as a success.

Chicken Florentine

Calla is a trained chef, but working with an extremely limited budget. She makes chicken florentine for Ian for their first date. This recipe will impress anyone without breaking the bank. It's delicious, hearty, and beautiful on the plate.

2 chicken breasts, skinned, boned, cut into halves

$^{1}/_{2}$ tsp salt (Kosher or sea salt is best)

$^{1}/_{4}$ tsp ground white pepper

1 TBS Extra virgin olive oil

$^{1}/_{2}$ cup chopped onion

$^{1}/_{2}$ cup chopped baby bella mushrooms

$^{1}/_{2}$ of 10 oz. pkg. frozen chopped spinach, thawed, well drained

$^{1}/_{3}$ cup ricotta cheese

A few grates of nutmeg (no more than $^{1}/_{4}$ tsp)

1 egg, lightly beaten

$^{1}/_{2}$ cup bread crumbs

Preparation

Slice the chicken breasts in half - like opening a book (so that you've reduced the thickness by half and not the length or width by half). Using a rolling pin or mallet, pound each half thin until about $^1/_3$ to $^1/_3$ inch thick. Sprinkle with salt and pepper.

Chop the onions.

Chop the mushrooms.

Place the thawed spinach in a towel and squeeze it dry.

Preheat oven to 350° degrees F (180° degrees C)

Beat egg.

Directions

Heat the olive oil in a skillet. Add the onions and mushrooms. Saute until onions are translucent, about 5-6 minutes.

Stir in the cheese and nutmeg. Stir just until heated.

Divide the mixture between the four breasts. Starting with the short end, roll up the breasts. (If necessary, you can secure them closed with wooden toothpicks.)

Dip each breast in the egg, then roll in breadcrumbs.

Place on baking pan, seam side down. Cover tightly

with aluminum foil.

Back at 350° degrees F (180° degrees C) for 15 minutes. Remove the foil covering and bake for an additional 10-15 minutes, or until browned.

French Bread

French bread is the perfect accompaniment to Chicken Florentine. It's a simple recipe and can easily be turned into garlic bread.

2 $^1/_4$ tsp (or 1 packet) dry years
1 $^1/_4$ cup warm filtered water no hotter than 120° degrees F (48° degrees C)
3 $^1/_2$ cups flour (I use fresh ground mixture of hard red wheat and hard white wheat - unbleached flour will work if you don't have fresh ground)
1 tsp salt (Kosher or sea salt is best)
1 TBS extra virgin olive oil

Preparation

Heat the mixing bowl by filling it with hot tap water.

Drain the bowl. Add the warm water and yeast. Let stand 5 minutes.

Lightly grease a large bowl to use for rising the dough.

Directions

Mix all ingredients in bowl with the water and yeast.

Knead with the stand mixer for 2 minutes, or knead by hand for 10 minutes.

Once the dough becomes smooth and elastic, put it into a lightly greased bowl. Turn it once and cover with a light towel. Let it sit in a warm spot until it doubles in bulk. It will take about an hour.

Punch the dough down. Roll dough into a rectangle and roll up tightly. Pinch the ends and place on a greased baking sheet (you can sprinkle the baking sheet with cornmeal if you desire). Cover and let rise in a warm place until nearly double in size.

Bake at 400° degrees F (205° degrees C) for 20-25 minutes. When you tap the loaf, if it sounds hollow, it's done.

Sauteed Green Beans

Even though the Spinach Florentine is stuffed with spinach, fresh green beans help the plate look like a work of art.

$^{1}/_{2}$ lb fresh green beans.

1 TBS extra virgin olive oil

1 clove garlic, minced

2 TBS sliced almonds

Wash the green beans. Cut off the stems.

Heat olive oil in skillet over medium-high heat. Add the garlic and saute for about 2 minutes, stirring constantly. Stir in the green beans and almonds.

Reduce heat to medium-low and cover the pan and cook for about 10 minutes, stirring the beans regularly.

Wild Rice

I use a packaged organic wild-rice and brown rice blend.

2 cups vegetable broth

1 cup wild-rice/brown rice blend

$^1/_2$ tsp salt

2 tsp extra virgin olive oil

In a medium saucepan, combine all ingredients. Bring to a boil. Cover pan tightly and reduce heat to low. Simmer for 45 minutes or until the brown rice is tender.

Basil Infused Whipped Cream

Calla wanted to serve a dessert that would be light and easy, but didn't want to serve "just plain" whipped cream. So, she infused her cream with basil and served that over berries.

Ingredients

1 cup heavy whipping cream

$^1/_3$ cup fresh basil leaves

1 TBS powdered sugar

Preparation

In a small saucepan, heat the cream over medium heat until almost boiling (do not boil) - just until it stars to simmer. Remove from heat and toss in the basil.

Sit at room temperature for 30 minutes. Strain the cream through a mesh strainer into a clean bowl. Refrigerate for at least 3 hours.

Directions

Mix the powdered sugar into the infused cream. Beat with a mixer until stiff peaks form.

Serve over fresh berries.

Find the latest information and connect with Hallee at her website: www.halleebridgeman.com

FICTION BOOKS BY HALLEE

The Jewel Series:

Book 1: Sapphire Ice
Book 2: Greater Than Rubies
Book 3: Emerald Fire
Book 4: Topaz Heat
Book 5: Christmas Diamond
Book 6: Christmas Star Sapphire
Book 7: Silver Hearts

The Song of Suspense Series:

Book 1: A Melody for James
Book 2: An Aria for Nick
Book 3: A Carol for Kent
Book 4: A Harmony for Steve

The Virtues and Valor series:
Book 1: Temperance's Trial
Book 2: Homeland's Hope
Book 3: Charity's Code
Book 4: A Parcel for Prudence
Book 5: Grace's Ground War
Book 6: Mission of Mercy
Book 7: Flight of Faith
Book 8: Valor's Vigil

Standalone Suspense:
On The Ropes

PARODY COOKBOOKS BY HALLEE

Fifty Shades of Gravy, a Christian gets Saucy!
The Walking Bread, the Bread Will Rise
Iron Skillet Man, the Stark Truth about Pepper and Pots
Hallee Crockpotter, & the Chamber of Sacred Ingredients

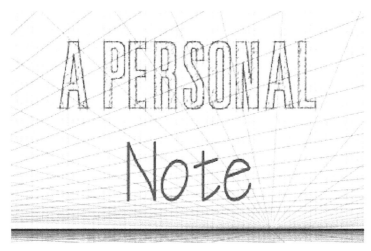

From Author Hallee Bridgeman

I can't tell you how thrilled I am to bring you this novella. When I was approached to write a story as part of the *Out of the Blue Bouquet* boxset, I knew I would make the story of Calla and Ian an introduction to the *Dixon Brothers Series*. It's always fun to begin a new series, to build a new world, and to have so many characters moving through that world.

As I wrote this book, I just hinted at the Dixons—a family with a set of triplet brothers who run one of the nation's largest contracting/architectural firms. When I originally came up with the idea for this set of stories, I managed the home office for a very successful general contractor in Florida, so construction projects were my world at the time. Because of that, every story in the Dixon Brothers Series holds a special place in my heart.

As for Calla and Ian, even though they have little interaction with the Dixons in this book, their story introduces readers to a cast of secondary characters who bring the world of thsi series such color and life that I know you will fall in love with every book.

The link to sign up for my newsletter is in the back of this book—make sure you sign up if you want to receive notifications with each release! As you read the books, please consider leaving honest reviews wherever you bought them. Honest reviews help other readers decide whether they want to fall in love with these stories as well!

May God bless you,

HALLEE BRIDGEMAN

www.halleebridgeman.com

With more than half a million
sales and more than 20 books in print,
Hallee Bridgeman is a best-selling
Christian author who writes romance
and action-packed romantic suspense
focusing on realistic characters who
face real world problems. Her work
has been described as everything
from refreshingly realistic to
heart-stopping exciting and edgy.

An Army brat turned Floridian, Hallee finally settled in central Kentucky with her family so she could enjoy the beautiful changing of the seasons. She enjoys the roller-coaster ride thrills that life with a National Guard husband, a daughter away at college, and two elementary aged sons delivers.

A prolific writer, when she's not penning novels, you will find her in the kitchen, which she considers the "heart of the home." Her passion for cooking spurred her to launch a whole food, real food "Parody" cookbook series. In addition to nutritious, Biblically grounded recipes, readers will find that each cookbook also confronts some controversial aspect of secular pop culture.

Hallee is a member of the Published Author Network (PAN) of the Romance Writers of America (RWA) where she serves as a long time board member in the Faith, Hope, & Love chapter. She is a member of the American Christian Fiction Writers (ACFW) and the American Christian Writers (ACW) as well as being a member of Novelists, Inc. (NINC).

Hallee loves coffee, campy action movies, and regular date nights with her husband. Above all else, she loves God with all of her heart, soul, mind, and strength; has been redeemed by the blood of Christ; and relies on the presence of the Holy Spirit to guide her. She prays her work here on earth is a blessing to you and would love to hear from you.

www.halleebridgeman.com

You can reach Hallee via the CONTACT link on her website or send an email to hallee@halleebridgeman.com.

Newsletter Sign Up: tinyurl.com/HalleeNews/

Author Site: www.halleebridgeman.com/

Facebook: www.facebook.com/pages/Hallee-Bridgeman/192799110825012

Twitter: twitter.com/halleeb

Google+: plus.google.com/105383805410764959843

Goodreads: www.goodreads.com/author/show/5815249.Hallee_Bridgeman

Homemaking Blog: www.halleethehomemaker.com

Sign up for Hallee's monthly newsletter! Sign up for Hallees monthly newsletter! When you sign up, you will get a link to download Hallee's romantic suspense novella, On The Ropes. In addition, every newsletter recipient is automatically entered into a monthly giveaway! The real prize is you will never miss updates about upcoming releases, book signings, appearances, or other events.

Hallee News Letter
http://tinyurl.com/HalleeNews/